DEDICATION

Men and women will lie with each other and that union sometimes brings forth a child. After that, some of those men and women actually become mothers and fathers. The union doesn't make it so: The dedication, courage, and responsibility to raise those children does, and to teach them love, morality, respect, beauty, and the art of survival; that is being a mother or father. To the single mother who works two jobs, refusing welfare and raising her children to grow up straight and tall; to the single father who struggles to love his children when a tangled system or angry ex tries to prevent that; to the husband and wife who think of the example they set for their children in every life decision they make; to the parents who stay together and work through the struggles of a marriage and teach their children about commitment; to those who hug and kiss their children but also have the courage to give them discipline, too; to those who always remember the love that brought forth their children; to my mother and father and to all those who are the real heroes, to those who are the real mothers and fathers, I dedicate this book.

—Don Bendell

Woman of My Youth

My winter count grows longer
As does the count of her,
The woman, the woman of my youth.
Father Time draws lines on her face;
Yet still, I see the beauty lying there.
Within those eyes are hidden secrets,
Secrets of love and life and faith;
And in the corners of those eyes
The imp of laughter still hides.
The legs and tummy are still so firm:
The breasts still soft, yet proud.
The mind is still as sharp but wiser now.
Her lips against mine are like so much;
The snow against the rock, the sea upon the sand,
Her pups are now grown wolves
Creating now their packs and mates.
Some days she looks back and cries.
But why? For she is the woman of my youth,
And more, more important still;
She will always be the woman of her youth.

I Love you, Shirley.
by Don Bendell from
Of Doves, Hawks, and Eagles

"The hand that rocks the cradle is the hand that rules the world."

—W. S. Ross

BACKGROUND:
THE COLT FAMILY

Chris Colt became famous as a chief of scouts for the U.S. Cavalry and was equally famous for his iron nerve and the speed and deadliness of his quick draw. Born to a cobbler in Cuyahoga Falls, Ohio and related to the famous Colonel Samuel Colt, young Chris would visit Uncle Samuel and was entranced by the gunsmiths at the famous factory back East. He started practicing quick draw secretly as a boy, and wanting adventure and excitement, he joined the 171st Regiment of the Ohio National Guard as a very young teenager and went off to fight for the Union Army in the Civil War, where Chris became a scout and started learning about courage, and developed tremendous stalking and tracking skills. Ohio held nothing for him after that, and he journeyed West, where he worked at many jobs before scouting for the cavalry. His abilities and reputation grew rapidly with each adventure, and he was soon a chief of scouts.

He also fell in love with a Minniconjou Lakotah (Sioux) woman named Chantapeta, for Fire

Heart, and they had a little girl named Winona, for First Born. Both were raped and murdered by four renegade Crow warriors, and the brokenhearted chief of scouts hunted down and killed each one.

Hired as chief of scouts for George Armstrong Custer, whom he could not stand, Chris Colt was befriended by the famous Lakotah warrior/chieftain Crazy Horse. Fired by Custer on the way to the Little Big Horn, Chris Colt was held and bound by Crazy Horse in the giant encampment during the Battle of the Little Big Horn, so he would not warn Custer or fight against the Lakotah, Cheyenne, and Arapaho. Sitting Bull had wisely warned Colt that he could never tell of his presence at the battleground or people would think he deserted Custer. At the same time, Crazy Horse had rescued the woman Colt fell in love with, Shirley Ebert of Bismarck, Dakota Territory who had been kidnapped by a giant of a man named Will Sawyer.

Chris Colt later hunted the man down, killing him in a fight in the Valley of the Yellowstone.

He married Shirley, and they had two children Joseph and Brenna, who were raised on Colt's ranch the Coyote Run. Shirley, ironically, had grown up in Youngstown, Ohio, not too far from Cuyahoga Falls. Chris and Shirley shared the sprawling ranch at the base of the Sangre de Cristo Mountains in the Wet Mountain Valley in southern Colorado, with Chris's older half brother Joshua Colt, who looked like a twin to Chris except with brown skin and black curly hair. The bastard son of a love union between Chris's dad and a slave, Joshua Colt had forgotten more about the cattle business and horses than most ranchers knew.

Colt ended up with Chief Joseph of the Nez Percé in their seventeen-hundred-mile fighting flight for freedom, which is still considered the greatest tactical fighting retreat of all time. It was also the first time that the press and public opinion took the side of the Indians, because Colt persuaded Chief Joseph not to attack civilians or take scalps. The cavalry on the other hand took Nez Percé scalps and killed women and children.

Colt and his young Nez Percé sidekick Man Killer also led the scouting for the all-black buffalo soldiers in their campaign against the feared Apache renegade leader Victorio.

After that, Chris Colt was made Deputy U.S. Marshal and deputized Man Killer to work for him. Man Killer married a Westcliffe beauty named Jennifer Banta, who inherited a fortune. Chris Colt's reputation and legend grew even larger as a deputy sheriff as did Man Killer's, especially when the young brave went so far as to have himself purposely shanghaied so he could sail to Australia to rescue his then-fiancée Jennifer, who had been taken off by a greedy uncle. Also growing in reputation, down in Texas, was Chris Colt's younger cousin Justis Colt, who was becoming famous as a Texas Ranger. He was always escorted by his mute, Comanche-trained sidekick, Tora, a former samurai from Japan.

Now another Colt had sprung up, Chris and Joshua's ravishing younger sister, Charley Colt, who was another love child of their father and a beautiful southern aristocrat.

Meconi still had that gold and Charley Colt had been working jobs dressed as a man so she could support her two little girls. At the same time, she had been hunting down the men who had betrayed and killed her husband.

CHAPTER 1

Mrs. Colt

The afternoon heat beat down on the flat rock along the banks of the crystal clear Texas Creek, which ran down from the glacial runoff of the Colorado Sangre de Cristo range. The rattlesnake was now eight years old, sporting ten rattles, the result of each skin's shedding. It left the warmth of the flat rock to search for food, although it was daytime and by instinct it did most of its hunting at night. Not far away a little boy and girl played and giggled but the snake was unable to hear or see them. If they were closer, the forked tongue would have picked up their movement, but they were across the yard from him when he slithered toward the large ranch house.

Shirley Colt wiped her hands on her apron after setting down the crocheted pot holders, a gift from Ellie Richards, a neighbor down the

Wet Mountain Valley who had been visited by Shirley after her husband died up on Music Pass during a late-spring snowstorm. Shirley Colt was the richest rancher in the valley and was the only one who seemed to really care, Ellie thought, because hers was one of the least prosperous ranches around.

Shirley looked at young Joseph and Brenna playing in the yard and smiled, then went to the library room in the big house that her husband, Chris, used as an office when he was home. Chris and his deputy, Man Killer, were off north somewhere, trying to solve a series of killings which had started with a freighter named James Adams, who had left a beautiful wife and two small daughters behind. Shirley only knew that there was a Pinkerton agent involved and there was some sort of U.S. government secret involved, too. Since her husband, the legendary chief of scouts/gunfighter-turned-lawman, Chris Colt, was a deputy U.S. marshal, naturally he was working on this important case.

To save him time, as she often did, Shirley sat down at the desk and started sorting the various telegrams and mail which had come in for him while he was out on the hunt.

At the same time, the buzztail, seeking a little cooler place to hunt, slithered up the steps, across the back porch, and into the kitchen, moving slowly along under the shadows of the cupboard doors. He curled up behind the fireplace utensils on the cooler fossilized rocks which made up the giant stone fireplace shared by the kitchen and dining room, one of two fireplaces in the house.

Shirley checked once on the children and saw them enter the barn then returned to her work in the office. Finishing that, she grabbed a quilt she had been working on for the church they attended in Westcliffe. The church wanted to raffle it off to raise money for a new building, so Shirley had been working on it during every spare moment. As she passed through the kitchen this time, the rattler picked up her vibrations and started to rattle, stopping her in midstride. She looked and listened but could not identify the brief sound, so Shirley went on to the porch.

She sat in her favorite spot, in the rocker Chris had had handmade for her out of elk antlers with velvet cushions by a craftsman up in Denver, one hundred and twenty miles to the north as the crow flies. There she could sit and work on the quilt while looking at the horses and cattle in the far-off pastures that rose slowly toward the thickets of scrub oak which dotted the foothills of the majestic mountain peaks that ascended above her and towered into the sky, the snow glistening off their glacial caps. She never tired of that view, or the one of her children playing in the large grassy backyard along the banks of Texas Creek, which traversed their property before making its way ten miles downhill and spilling into the tumbling, churning, foamy Arkansas River.

The thought hit Shirley that she hadn't seen Joseph and Brenna for a little bit, so she set down her handiwork and walked quietly toward the barn. As she approached, she heard the sounds of an argument from within. Sneaking up to one of the large windows, Shirley peered in and saw Joseph on a bale of bedding straw, his nose scrunched and knees drawn up under his arms.

He was obviously upset. Brenna, his junior by a couple of years, was chanting, "Joseph is a scaredy-cat, and 'fraid to fight the bullies. Joseph is a scaredy-cat, and 'fraid to fight the bullies."

Joseph defiantly and angrily said, "Am not."

Shirley quickly retreated back to her rocker and thought the matter over, trying to decide best how to handle it. She went back inside to build a fire so she could swing the big iron arm and cooking pot over it where she would make a giant pot of her famous beef stew. The children loved it, and Chris especially did. Maybe he would be home soon, and would enjoy a gallon or so down his throat. Shirley smiled as she thought how that big man could eat.

As she bent to grab the fireplace poker, the rattle made her stop in midmove. There was no halfway about it this time. The big snake was right in front her, curled up and ready to strike. Shirley did not hold with the old theory of not moving when a snake was ready to strike. Her hand jerked back and the snake lashed out, missing her by a foot. She grabbed the poker and yanked it back as he struck again.

After this strike however, as his upper body stretched out across the rocks, she pinned his head down with the poker and calmly reached down and grabbed him behind the deadly diamond-shaped head. Dropping the poker, she grabbed the rest of his body with her other hand and started for the door, but stopped, and turned, retracing her steps.

She tossed the snake down on the fireplace and ran over to the door, just in time to see her children emerge from the barn. Shirley screamed at the top of her lungs and smiled as she saw the two race across the yard, the eldest in the lead.

Shirley smiled and whispered to herself,

"Shirley Colt, you're crazy putting your son in harm's way like this."

Joseph burst through the door, a hastily grabbed rail-splitter in his hands. He looked at Shirley wide-eyed, and she feigned panic as she pointed at the fireplace. Joseph looked and stuck his shoulders back.

He gulped a little then said, "Shucks, Ma, it's just an old rattlesnake. Don't be scared. I'll catch him alive and give him to Tex. He'll make a dandy hatband out of him. Just a minute."

As Brenna ran in the door and saw the snake, Joseph ran past her, going outside.

Shirley held Brenna and said, "Your brother is so brave."

Joseph reentered the house, carrying a large forked stick and within tense minutes, he pinned the snake's head down and grabbed it safely behind the head.

He carried it out the door, and Shirley acted so relieved, saying over and over, "Thank you, Joseph. You're so brave."

When he came back, Shirley gave him a big hug and Brenna ran up to him and hugged him as hard as she could.

Shirley said, "Brenna, I believe you and I should make your big brother a pie. What kind do you want, Mr. Colt?"

Brenna giggled and Joseph threw his shoulders back a little more, smiling broadly. "How about apple, Ma?"

She winked at him and he walked over and hugged her again, saying, "You're the best Ma in the whole world."

She laughed and said, "You're only saying that because it's true."

All three started chuckling.

CHAPTER 2
A New Beginning

Charlotte Colt was a ravishing woman, and she had just come face-to-face with her famous older brother and couldn't bring herself to tell him who she was. He noticed her. Every man who laid eyes on her always saw her and most dreamed about her. But she saw Ezekiel Park, another one of the men who had murdered her husband, and ran from the train she was on to change into the clothing that hid her beauty. She changed into the character which had allowed her to support her two little girls ever since her husband had been shot. Charlotte with her breasts bound and her honey-dipped golden tresses beneath a Stetson and her makeup gone, was now Charley Anderson, the young man who had held a number of jobs receiving the wages that men were paid. She carefully jumped a boxcar on the northbound train she had spotted the killer in. Her brother U.S. Deputy Marshal Chris Colt and his deputy, Man Killer, the Nez Percé millionaire, were still on the southbound train where she had left them so abruptly.

In the other train, Colt looked at Man Killer and asked, "What is going on, little brother?"

Man Killer said, "I am reading a faint trail, but it gets sharper. If we want to discover the killer, we should follow her wherever she goes."

Chris Colt knew enough about Man Killer to listen to the young man's intuition.

He said, "You think she boarded the other train? In a dress and hoops?"

Man Killer said, "I was watching her pretty face. She saw something or some person out the window. Her mind is stalked by the great cat. She tries to decide if she should climb a tree, run, or stand and fight."

Chris stood up and said, "I'm trusting you on this. Come on."

Man Killer followed while Chris found the porter.

He said, "How long do we have to get our horses off here and switch to the northbound train?"

The porter said, "You has bouts five minutes, Marshal. I heps you."

A few minutes later, they loaded their horses

in one of the back cars and climbed in themselves, as there were no passenger cars. The brakeman offered to let them ride in the caboose, but they declined, saying that they wanted to ride in the boxcar with their horses. In actuality, they did not see Charlotte going anywhere and a quick look for tracks leading away from the train revealed none. The other train had already pulled out, and she was not on it.

Ezekiel Park climbed into the boxcar, quietly, and the train pulled out of the siding. The binding came loose around Charley's breasts, so, not hearing him, Charlotte quickly removed her homespun shirt and unwound the cloth around her bosom. At a sound behind her she suddenly spun around. Charley gasped as she looked into the evil, grinning face of Ezekiel Park. She covered her breasts with her hands and took a step backward.

"Well, well, well," he said, deep bass voice booming from his massive chest, "the little man is really a woman. Never know what I'm gonna find checkin' the cars. Looks like I'm gonna have some fun tonight."

He walked forward slowly, menacingly. Charley could feel her pulse beating in the sides of her neck. His fingers started unfastening his belt buckle. Watching him, Charley couldn't breathe. She couldn't swallow. As she stepped back a few more steps, her face was lit by a streak of moonlight. Recognition flashed on Ezekiel's face, and his look turned grave.

Her mind raced, then she pictured the man she had just met; her brother, Chris Colt. She thought about her other brother, Joshua, and the stories she had heard about him. She thought about her sister-in-law, Shirley Colt, and her courage, and Man Killer, who was essentially part of the Colt family. She thought about the uncle she never knew, Colonel Samuel Colt, and the tremendous impact he had had on the American West. Suddenly, Charley's attitude changed. She thought about the legacy of those Colts who had gone before her.

Charlotte steeled herself. Her shoulders went back. She even smiled as she dropped her hands.

Ezekiel froze in his tracks, staring at her breasts. He said, "Yer Mrs. Adams."

She said, "And you are one of the demons who murdered my husband."

He grinned but seemed nervous now and not the cocky person he had been seconds before.

He said, "What? Ain't scared all of a sudden?"

Charlotte grinned. "Why should I be? I'm the one with the gun on my hip."

He took a step forward. "But you ain't gonna murder an innocent man in cold blood. You can't kill me. You're just a tiny woman, but you shore have nice big titties."

"When you get to hell, tell your friends a tiny woman with big titties sent you there."

He took one more step, a little more cautiously, but Ezekiel Park was grinning fully now.

He said, "If you kill me, it's murder."

She drew and fired. The bullet caught him full in the stomach and knocked him back two steps. He was shocked, totally, and he grabbed his belly, blood pouring out between his fingers.

She said, "I think not. It's self-defense, and retribution. You helped murder my husband in cold blood."

Charley fanned her gun, and he went backward with each bullet—slamming into his stomach, chest, and upper thigh. He stood in the door of the boxcar, weaving on wobbly legs with blood running out his mouth and nose. His eyes opened wide as Charley holstered her .44 and walked toward him confidently.

In total shock, he looked at the blood dripping

off his hands, saying, "They're gonna hang ya. Ya murdered me."

Charley grinned sadistically, saying, "Murder? You would have raped me. I say it's self-defense."

Reaching him, his left arm came up feebly to try to grab her.

She ignored it and raised her leg, saying, "It's also justice." With that, she kicked him in the chest as hard as she could, and he flew out into the night air, landing on his back next to the tracks.

She looked back at his body and noticed movement about ten cars back. Chris Colt and Man Killer were not only looking at the body as they passed by but they were looking up at her face. She only had her head out of the car, so they didn't see her chest, and she still had her hat on. They disappeared back into their own car, then seconds later crawled out the door and started along the boxcar toward her car.

Charley ducked inside her car and quickly bound her breasts again and replaced her shirt. Her mind raced. The train was going slow now, very slow, as it was nearing the summit of Monument Pass, as it headed north toward Denver, from where she had left earlier. She was still not ready to disclose her secret identity; not until she got to Drago.

Man Killer and Chris were going to try to do their best to reach the car where the killer was hiding. First, by crawling along their car to the ladder, then going up on the rooftops.

Man Killer yelled, "Shoot," as he saw the little killer jump out and somersault into the grass along the tracks.

Luggage bag in hand, the little man came up running and Colt and Man Killer saw Charley closely as they passed by. They tried to make it back to the door as quickly as they could. Charley ran right at the freight, and they watched her as they continued on. Suddenly, as the front wheels passed, she dived under a car.

The two men made it into the boxcar and were thankful their horses were already saddled. They mounted up and waited for the train to make the top of the pass, where it would be moving its slowest. Colt sat in the door first, aiming his horse on an angle north so he could hit the ground, running. Both horses sensed battle and were ready to go.

The train slowed even more and Colt touched his heels and calves to War Bonnet's flanks and the big paint dived into the night air. They indeed hit the ground, running, and he pulled up to wait for Man Killer, but Hawk misstepped, going out the door, and hit the ground straight-legged. It jarred the big Appaloosa, but Man Killer went sailing over his head and hit his head on a rock. Colt had started to chase after the train, as he knew immediately what had happened. Charley had simply dived under the train, rolled out between the wheels, on the far side, and climbed up into one of the other box-cars near the end of the train. He would easily overtake the slow-moving train, however.

Colt looked back and saw the empty saddle of Hawk and the prone shadow in the grass.

"Son of a!" he yelled, slapping his hat on his leg.

Chris wheeled his horse and loped back to his fallen amigo, jumping down. Man Killer moaned as Colt lifted his head.

Charlotte looked back out the door of the box-car and saw what had happened, then saw Man Killer slowly getting to his feet with the help of the big marshal. The train over the summit now started picking up speed, and she breathed a sigh of relief. The two men slowly mounted up and rode back toward the body, as the train disappeared from sight, heading north.

Man Killer made a fire next to the tracks from sticks and brush nearby. They inspected the body of the black man and pulled out two sketches they received from the Pinkerton man. One sketch was taken from a tintype of Drago Meconi. The other was a sketch of Ezekiel from an old wanted poster. His pockets revealed nothing but an old stopwatch with someone else's name engraved on it.

Colt said, "That little guy is killing off Meconi's gang, except I have some news for you about him. He is a she."

Man Killer said, "How do you know for sure?"

Colt said, "We were suspicious before, so I looked closely. When she ran by us, I couldn't see her face. By the way, when we check her tracks, I'll guarantee that they match the ones by Cyrus Minty's death scene."

He rolled a cigarette and lit it in the fire.

Colt continued, "Anyway, when she ran by, I did get a clear look at her neck, and she didn't have an Adam's apple. Men have Adam's apples and women don't."

Man Killer took a swallow from his canteen and handed it to Colt.

The Nez Percé seemed hesitant about responding. He cleared his throat.

Man Killer said, "That is not all."

Colt asked, "What else?"

Man Killer said, "That woman. We know now she is the small man we saw who shot this one. That woman is the sister that old freight driver in New Mexico told you about. She is your sister."

The cigarette literally fell out of Colt's mouth, and he said, "What?"

Man Killer said, "Do you remember in the saloon in Westcliffe when you first met your brother, Joshua?"

Colt nodded, flashing back to the time he and Man Killer found three hardcases bracing a lone black man in the saloon. Chris Colt thought he was looking into a dirty mirror.

The man seated at the table in the corner had a grin on his face while the three tough-looking gunslingers stood over his table, all holding six-shooters in their hands.

What was amazing was that the rough-looking man at the table had light brown skin and black, very curly hair, but other than that, he looked very much like Christopher Columbus Colt. Almost identical in fact.

He was definitely a man of the range. Colt could spot that immediately. The man wore a beat-up, but clean and oiled, classic walnut-handled Colt .45 Peacemaker. His light brown holster and gunbelt were scuffed and scarred from many days and nights on the trail. His batwing leather chaps looked the same. Like Colt, he wore fancy big-roweled Mexican spurs, but each had two tiny little brass bells which made tiny tinkling sounds when he walked or rode, as they slapped up against the metal spurs. He wore a faded red western bib shirt, and it was apparent, like Chris Colt, the large shirt did little to hide large bulging chest muscles and shoulders, hardened by many hours of hard work. A large cowboy's scarf was tied around his neck with a slip knot, the habit of wise western working men not desirous of being accidentally lynched when their horse passed under a low-hanging tree branch. The left side of his gunbelt held a large bowie knife. The black man had an ivory toothpick sticking out between his white teeth and Colt could see that the end of it had been carved into the shape of a Colt .45. It looked very familiar.

Man Killer looked at the man and stared, eyes-wide, then turned and stared at Colt.

Man Killer said, "Colt, he is your brother!"

Learning of Joshua was very traumatic for Chris, and now Colt was trying to deal with having a sister.

He snuffed out his cigarette and chuckled to himself. Man Killer looked over at him.

Chris explained, "Some men love to go fishing. Some like to go to saloons and drink or play faro, poker, or blackjack. Some men just whittle or some like making furniture. I never knew it, but I guess my old man had his own hobby."

Man Killer laughed and replied, "He was very busy with it."

Both men laughed.

They buried Ezekiel Park and waited for the next northbound train. Man Killer tried to ignore his headache. When they finally arrived in Castle Rock, they disembarked and headed for the saloon. Charley had bought a ticket, or at least a small man had, and was headed back to Santa Fe. The two men had a few hours to kill before the next train south, so they decided to have a beer.

Man Killer pointed at every man that walked in the saloon for two hours and asked Colt if that man might be Colt's brother also.

Two days later, Man Killer and Chris Colt were the objects of many stares, especially by women as they rode through the streets of Santa Fe, Spanish-influenced architecture almost everywhere. It was midafternoon and siesta time, so there was hardly any movement anywhere. Chris and Man Killer also figured it would be the best time to locate Charlotte, whether dressed as a man or a woman, because the only people stirring, chances were, would be the non-residents of Santa Fe. Even the non-Hispanic residents of Santa Fe observed siesta time each day.

Their strategy was simple; Colt and Man Killer started riding up and down the main streets and side streets of Santa Fe, looking for either a woman or a man who looked like the person who had sat with Chris Colt on the train.

Chris Colt had a great deal of pride and he had the same pride in his family as well. It was very difficult for him to imagine that his sister would be a killer, even if she was raised by a totally different family.

Colt and Man Killer were riding slowly down the street when the town marshal came around the block on a beautiful palomino gelding. Riding a high-backed Mexican saddle and donning a brown derby on his bald head, the marshal trotted up to the federal lawmen and doffed his hat.

"You'll be Marshal Colt," he said. "I'm John Troop. Got a telygram fer ya from a Pinkerton named Ferruccio. Says it's important."

Colt examined the telegram. "Drago Meconi has purchased a mining operation in Denver, and Piney Waters is his foreman. He's been drinking and gambling in Denver and hiring a bunch of toughs." He looked up at Man Killer. "What do you say we ride?"

The two disembarked from the train in Pueblo and took the first train headed west toward Canon City. They unloaded at Canon City, as the tracks were down in the Arkansas River canyon, due to a rockslide across the tracks.

Learning about the rockslide, Man Killer said, "We could get someone to take us up the tracks to Spike Buck and ford the Arkansas there. Then we go up Spike Buck Gulch. We have to lead the horses through the narrows and tie our stirrups up on the saddles, but it will be shorter. We cross south of Lookout Mountain and come out in Likely Gulch and take the Texas Creek Road to the ranch."

Chris said, "The rockslide is at Pinnacle Rock, so maybe we can if I pay someone enough to haul us up there and then take the train all the way back to Canon City."

After arranging a train which would leave in an hour, the two men went to the Canon City Hot Springs near the depot. Single baths were advertised for a dollar and tickets could be bought for four dollars and fifty cents per dozen.

They had been here many times before. They had a sign on the wall which read:

AMONG THE DISEASES IN WHICH THE MOST MARKED BENEFIT HAS BEEN NOTICED BY USE OF THE BATH, MAY BE MENTIONED RHEUMATISM, CUTANEOUS DISEASES, CATARRH, TORPIDITY OF THE LIVER, DISEASES OF THE KIDNEYS, AND ALL SCROFULOUS AFFECTIONS.

THE SPRINGS HAVE ONE OF THE FINEST SANITARY LOCATIONS IN COLORADO. THE ALTITUDE BEING ABOUT FIVE THOUSAND FEET (NEARLY TWO THOUSAND FEET LESS THAN ANY OTHER HOT SPRINGS IN THE STATE). THEY OFFER TO THE NEWCOMER AN ESPECIAL ADVANTAGE, AS IT IS NOT SAFE OR DESIRABLE FOR INVALIDS TO GO IMMEDIATELY INTO A HIGH ALTITUDE.

There was also a sign on the wall which read:

"OF ALL THE MINERAL WATERS OF THE WEST WHICH I HAVE ANALYZED, I FIND THOSE OF CANON CITY THE BEST." PROFESSOR LOWE, THE WHEELER EXPEDITION.

There was also a chart on the wall showing the percentage of grains of various minerals per gallon of water. Still another stated that the constant temperature of the water was 104 degrees.

An hour later, they were aboard a two-car freight train headed west toward the whitewater Arkansas River. It was later in the summer, and the river was not as high as it was in June from the snow melt-up in the Collegiate Range and the Sangre de Cristos. Some summers the bridges were washed out in June, but now the river could even be forded in a couple of places if a horse had strong legs and wasn't prone to panic.

When the refreshed pair arrived in Denver, they were not alone. After Joshua Colt heard what had happened, he turned the ranch operation over to Tex Westchester, his grizzled, old top hand.

Joshua said simply, "She's my sister, too. I'm going with you."

Shirley and the kids kissed Chris, then they each hugged Man Killer and Joshua and the trio left for Cotopaxi to catch the early-morning east-bound to Pueblo. From there, they would go north to Denver.

It was two in the morning and Charlotte Colt Adams, dressed as Charley Anderson, had been drinking and watching Drago Meconi and Piney Waters playing poker for some hours now. They were in a saloon not far from Cherry Creek. The killer had purchased the successful Crooked Sister Mining Company, west of Denver, from an Eastern concern, and he'd also bought a smaller mine, and a stage line that operated all along the Front Range from Trinidad to Fort Collins.

Charlotte had no idea where he got the money for the purchases, but all of a sudden he did. She heard about the mining operation and the stage line from freighters she had talked to in Santa Fe, and she boarded the first train north. Her daughters were doing fine, and she loved seeing them, but she had a task to finish.

In Denver, Charley Colt, as herself, met someone she thought she would never ever meet. Her name was Sadie Liekens, and she was a nice woman approaching middle age, with blue eyes and light brown curly hair put up on her head. Sadie Liekens was making history, as she was a woman police officer hired by the Denver Police Department. It was an experiment in social change, and Sadie actually would end up spending ten years as a dedicated officer with the department.

Charlotte said, "I have so much respect for you for becoming a police officer. You must get harassed terribly."

Sadie replied, "I do, but I knock them into shape if I have to."

Charley chuckled and Sadie went on. "Seriously, you would be pleased to know that we also have a woman lawyer, who does quite well in the courtroom, and she was just admitted to the American Bar Association."

Charley said, "That is wonderful. I never heard that. What is her name?"

Sadie replied, "Mary Lathrop."

Charlotte said, "I'm glad that some people are figuring out that half of our population can also make a contribution to society."

Sadie smiled, "That is nothing, Charlotte." She looked around to insure there were no eavesdroppers and continued in a low voice, "I was contacted by a woman in Rawlings, Wyoming, named Lillian Heath. She had heard about me and wanted to let me know she has been dressing like a man and is learning medicine from the town doctor. She is planning on becoming an obstetrician. Can you imagine that, though. She is actually getting away with posing as a man and even carries pistols in holsters. Can you imagine that?"

Charlotte said, "Yes, I can. It's just a shame that a woman would have to do such a thing just to make money or be dedicated to a profession."

Sadie said, "You are sure right there, but it's up to women like us to lead the way, isn't it?"

Charlotte nodded affirmatively and said, "But it certainly is a man's world."

Sadie grinned, saying, "That's all right. We shall simply let the men keep thinking that, while we do what God has divined for us to do."

Charley felt a twinge of guilt when Sadie referred to God, but Charley reasoned that her husband's soul would not rest until his killers were brought to justice, and she could just not fathom why nobody had even investigated his death. She almost confessed to Sadie about her own double life when she mentioned Lillian Health, but Charley thought better of it.

She spoke with Sadie about Drago Meconi and learned what saloons he hung out at, and also learned that money certainly hadn't made him any less of a brute.

Two nights later, she found him in the saloon where she now was.

Meconi was drinking heavily and playing poker. He was very boisterous and demanding. He had several hangers-on soaking up some of the money he was laying out. Charley blended in with that group. She wasn't sure what she would do, but eventually a plan came to her. Piney Waters and the others started dwindling away, and Charlotte went out back to the outbuilding and loosened the binding around her breasts.

A half hour later, when the game broke, Drago was well into his cups. Charley accompanied him as he left the building, and they made their way down the dark Denver street.

Drago looked over at Charley and said, "So where do I know you from, little guy? Was your name Charley, did you say?"

Charlotte said, "Yes, Charley. I know you from freighting. I'm a teamster."

"The hell you say," he slurred. "A little guy like you can handle a team and a load? Yer kinda a cute little guy. Ever been with a man before?"

Charlotte was shocked, but she followed him into an alleyway. He pulled his suspenders off his shoulders.

Unbuttoning her shirt, Charlotte said, "Yes, I have. My husband."

He did a double take and said, "What?"

Charley said, "My husband, James Adams! The man you murdered!"

His eyes opened wide like saucers, and he said, "You can't, ah, yer a woman!"

Charley pulled her binding off her breasts, and they both fell out. She clawed for her gun as the drunken Meconi stared in shock at her bosom.

He suddenly realized that she was about to shoot him, and he lashed out, backhanding her across the face just as she fired. The bullet took the tip of Drago's ear off, but she didn't see that. She went sprawling to the ground.

Holding his bloody ear, Drago pulled out his piece and fired at the prone figure. The bullet splashed muddy water into Charley's face, blinding her temporarily. She rolled madly away from the shots as he kept shooting and missing her. She fired again, barely able to see him. The bullet spun him around, taking him in the left shoulder.

She kept rolling and heard his gun click on an empty cylinder. He muttered a curse and took off running. Charlotte heard police whistles in the distance and several dogs barking. She quickly made her way out the end of the alleyway, buttoning her shirt on the way. No one saw her before she reached the small boarding room where she was staying. Meconi wasn't getting away, though, she thought darkly. She'd go after him the next day, and this time she'd finally make him pay.

Charlotte Colt had on a man's red western shirt, but this morning her breasts were not bound underneath. She also wore women's riding boots over her denims, and her .44 was low-slung in a holster on her right hip. She had another .44 Russian tucked into her waistband.

She finished with her makeup and brushed out her beautiful blond hair.

An hour later, the hired buggy dropped her off at the entrance of the Crooked Sister Mine. She had no plan. She was just angry that this man who had killed her husband was rich, while she was separated from her daughters, and her husband lay in a grave. She knew that the Colt blood flowed through her veins, and she was going to confront Drago Meconi head-on just as her famous brothers would.

Charley was surprised that the guard at the main gate allowed her to pass right through. Going forward cautiously, she rounded a long building that looked like a warehouse. The mine shaft was directly in front of her with little tracks coming out from a foothill. In the background, a snow-capped range loomed in the sky.

All at once men started pouring out of the mine. The last one was Drago Meconi, with his left arm in a sling and his shoulder heavily bandaged. Piney Waters stood at his side. The men spread apart, all armed, and walked ten abreast toward the lone gun woman.

Charlotte was scared, but she was also angry and determined. Her mind raced for a way to throw them off balance.

She said, "All you men just to kill one woman? My, how brave."

That remark made several shuffle nervously, and one man even started walking away.

He said, "She's right. I've done a lot a bad things in mah time, but I ain't no woman killer."

Drago didn't say a word. He simply drew and fired. The man flew backward, bits of skull and brain preceding his flight.

Drago said, "Any more deserters?"

He stared at the man's body, then added, "Right between the eyes. I'm not drunk today, Mrs. Adams."

Charlotte said, "It is Mrs. Colt-Adams, and I'm not drunk either."

The name Colt was added for effect, and she could tell several took notice. She accepted that she was going to die. She just wanted an edge so she could at least take Meconi and Waters with her.

Waters chuckled and said, "Drago said you'd show up. Mebbe we'll let ya live ef'n ya start gittin shut a them clothes and show us all what ya showed Drago."

Charley heard a noise from in back of her but didn't dare turn around. Some men were walking behind her, and she could see the men she confronted all looking.

Desperately, she said, "Drago, I know my husband gave you a job and paid you well. You, too, Waters. And you paid him back with bullets in the back. Now before your backshooters behind me kill me, I want you to know you and Piney are going with me."

A steely voice behind her said, "We aren't backshooters. We are your family." For the benefit of the others, the voice yelled, "And if you come up against one Colt, you come up against all of them."

Chris Colt stepped up next to Charley to her left and smiled at her.

He said softly, "Hello, little sister."

Joshua stepped up on her right side, saying, "Hello, Charlotte, I'm your big brother Joshua."

Man Killer popped up from behind rocks near the mine, a rifle in his hands.

"I, too, am family, Charlotte. I am Man Killer."

The outlaws all winced when they heard him behind them.

Eyes glistening, Charley smiled at her two brothers and Man Killer.

Chris Colt said, "Drago Meconi, I am Deputy U.S. Marshal Chris Colt. This is my brother and deputy, Joshua Colt. Behind you is my deputy, Man Killer. You and Piney Waters are under arrest for stealing an army payroll in excess of two million dollars and for murdering my brother-in-law, James Adams, who was carrying that payroll."

She yelled, "Hey, Drago, remember last night when I was dressed up just like a man, and you thought I was one. Why don't you tell your hired guns there how you asked me to have sex with you?"

His face turned beet red, the veins in his face and neck bulging out. His head started vibrating with rage.

His hand streaked down, but not before her .44 blossomed flame. He clutched the red stain on his midsection.

Guns started going off, and she heard Chris yell, "Joshua, right side!"

The three Colts walked forward, fanning and hammering shots into the melee with would-be gunhands falling in front of them. Piney Waters had drawn and was taking careful aim at Charlotte when his face disappeared in an explosion of blood and matter from Man Killer's shot. There was a lull in the shooting, and everything seemed to stop.

Drago looked at the half-dozen bullet holes in him and stared at Charley, saying, "You're just a woman!"

Chris yelled, "That's for sure. She's also a Colt!"

Drago's eyes glazed over, and he pitched forward on his face. The two outlaws still standing dropped their guns. Man Killer climbed down off the cliff and started gathering their guns and rounding them up. Several more lay on the ground, moaning. Most of them weren't moving at all.

Charley turned to her brothers, tears running down her high beautiful cheekbones.

Chris said, "Well, Shirley ought to be on a train about now taking your daughters back to our ranch."

Charley cried even more and was totally shocked.

She said, "But why?"

Joshua said, "Well, Charlotte, because you own part of it. You're a Colt, aren't you?"

She grabbed both men in a big hug and said, "Yes, I am. I am a Colt and proud of it, and by the way, call me Charley."

Chris said, "Call us family. We're matched Colts."

A big smile on her face, Charley started sobbing and was comforted in the arms of her two big brothers. The door to the mysterious little room in her life finally closed, and she was now complete. At long last, Charley had her family; a family that would go down in infamy. Their name was Colt, and now she and her daughters would have a home, a loving home with family. She had heard of the big beautiful Coyote Run Ranch near Westcliffe and now she would raise her daughters there, where they would have uncles and an aunt and friends. There was a lot of catching up to do and she would start to do it on the train ride home the next day.

CHAPTER 3

A Mother's Courage

Shirley Colt had a quiet dignity about her, although she was friendly to everyone. Her beauty was not only in her green eyes and auburn hair, her athletic figure, and warm smile; it was an inner beauty. She had had a successful restaurant in Bismarck when she met Chris. Her cooking was second to none, and her establishment had always been filled.

Yet ever since Shirley had met Chris, she had wanted one thing in life and that was to be his wife and the mother of his children. She could have gone on being a success, but her heart was in what she was doing right now. She loved her life on the frontier, the untamed West.

In the mornings, clutching a steaming cup of coffee, she loved to walk out onto the porch and sit in the swing and just look up at the fourteen-thousand-foot peaks that loomed over her home.

The timberline was somewhere around eleven thousand feet and covered the big range with an emerald carpet that gave way to the almost year-round snowcaps on the big peaks. The colors on the snow and the blue of the sky and swirling clouds were breathtaking in the mornings and the evenings. The Spanish Conquistadors had christened these mountains the Sangre de Cristos, which means the Blood of Christ, because of the crimson hues on the snowcaps at sunrise.

All four children had played hard all morning, after chores, and were now napping, while Shirley looked up at the peaks and enjoyed her coffee. She was at peace with the world, and she thought about Chris and his siblings returning from Silver Cliff. Chris had been like a little boy for the past month since he had brought his sister home to the ranch. Joshua was just as bad.

The three Colts, Chris, Joshua, and Charley, were now in Silver Cliff with the ranch's top hand, Tex Westchester, and they each drove a large freight wagon, which was all loaded with building supplies for Charley's new home they were building. People in the town stared at the golden-haired beauty and were as amazed at her ability to handle a big freight wagon as they were entranced by her looks. Having learned from witnessing many experiences with their famous neighbors, nobody was really shocked though. This gorgeous woman was, after all, Chris and Joshua Colt's sister. Nobody knew that she was another bastard sibling to Chris Colt, but just assumed that they had lived together as children. Shirley liked Charley very much when she met her, and she absolutely adored her new nieces. They were great playmates for her own daughter, Brenna and, of course, her oldest, Joseph, named for the famous Nez Percé chief, had instantly matured as the oldest, with two younger female cousins to look over now, as well as Brenna. The young man was already showing glimpses of the greatness he was inheriting, though still a young pup.

He had been given a magnificent gelding for his seventh birthday by Man Killer and his wife, Jennifer. The horse, a white leopard Appaloosa with roan spots all over its body, could run like the wind. Joseph had named him Spot, much to the amusement of his family. Each day he rode the horse to school bareback. Shirley and Chris had argued about this, but Shirley told him that Joseph would become an outstanding horseman if they made him ride bareback for his first year. He would be forced to learn how the hold the horse's sides with his calves and use leg aids to help reining. He would also develop a rhythm and balance with the horse.

One day, a week after his father and Charley had come home, Joseph rode up to school, and turned his horse loose in the little corral out back. Two bullies, both a head taller than him and two years older, started teasing him about being so short. When Joseph ignored them, this seemed to egg them on even more. Although he refused to be intimidated, they kept up their taunting all day.

That afternoon, when he left the one-room schoolhouse, one of the two tripped him as he walked out the door. Joseph fell headlong down the steps, bumping and cutting his right eyebrow. It immediately began swelling. Joseph Colt jumped to his feet and faced his antagonists, fists doubled.

One of them, Jim-Bob, said, "Ya little runt. What ya think yer gonna do, whip us?"

Joseph was frightened, but he didn't show it. He was the son of Chris and Shirley Colt. He set his jaw against the shaking he felt inside.

He answered the bully, "There's two of you and you're bigger than me, but I'm going to fight you. If I have to take twenty licks to hit each of you once, I'll do it."

The two bullies looked at each other, grinning,

and Joseph dived headfirst into the belly of Jim-Bob, driving the larger boy back onto his rear. The wind left Jim-Bob in a rush. Joseph turned in time to take a punch to the jaw from the other, Walter. The fight was on then. Joseph barreled into the stomach of Walter, to the admiring cheers of all the other students.

Joseph Colt fought like a tiger, even though he felt his right eye swelling shut. Nothing was going to stop him now. His arms were pinned behind his back by Jim-Bob while Walter started to pound him. Joseph stuck his right leg back behind him and hooked the leg of Jim-Bob, who was restraining him. He pushed backward with all his might and Jim-Bob tripped and fell, with Joseph landing on top of him. As soon as they hit the ground, Joseph drove his head backward into the bully's face. The older boy grabbed his bleeding nose and began crying.

Walter came at Joseph with a rush. Joseph jumped up to meet his charge, but immediately dropped into a ball. The bigger boy tripped over him and sprawled on top of his buddy. Joseph sprang on Walter in a flash and grabbed the boy's hair and yanked his head back. Wrapping his arm around the boy's neck, Joseph squeezed for all he was worth. Walter tried to stand, but Joseph wrapped his legs around the bully's waist and held tight. The harder the gasping bully struggled, the harder Joseph squeezed his arms around the boy's throat.

Finally, the boy, barely audible, cried out, "Uncle! Uncle!"

Joseph, however, wouldn't let go right away, saying, "You promise?"

The boy, face bright red and clearly panicked now, exclaimed, "Yes, I swear!"

Joseph let go, and the boy rose to his feet slowly, rubbing his throat, and went to the well to get a dipper full of water. He drank and choked and poured the dipper on his head. Jim-Bob, sporting a bloody nose, joined him at the well and tried cold water on his face to stop the bleeding, to no avail.

That's when the schoolteacher appeared. The three boys didn't know, but she had been watching from within the schoolhouse the whole time. She knew if anyone had a chance of teaching the bigger boys a lesson, it would be Joseph Colt.

The incident was also spotted by a pair of shifty eyes. They alternated between the fight in the schoolhouse yard, a stone's throw away, and the little bear cub being whittled by his own skilled leathery hands. The dark brown skin around his eyes was wrinkled from watching too many backtrails; first, watching for slave chasers and later watching for angry posses. The man had an ever-present smile on his face which was the result of a puckered cheek at the corner of both lips, where a panther had caught and torn both cheeks from the edges of his mouth when he was but a toddler in the far-off land called Africa. His father had dispatched the cat quickly enough, but two days later, the boy and the rest of his family were captured and taken off to America by slave traders. The man was buffalo-hide tough, and he saw the same in the young Colt boy. The man leaned back against the building, whittling on his bear cub until Joseph finally mounted up on Spot and headed back home for the ranch. The former slave then disappeared inside the nearby saloon, where he had left his partners, to make his report.

Joseph was very sore as the big horse trotted toward his home. He was usually comfortable trotting, even bareback, and felt at one with the horse. Passing Copper Gulch Road, he squeezed the horse's ribs with his calves. He temporarily forgot his aches and pains as Spot stretched out in a lope, and the wind whipped at his face. The horse loved to run, and the boy loved the feel of the speed and the thundering hooves. As they passed Reed Gulch, he finally pulled the horse back to an easy trot.

Joseph was dreaming about the bully incident and his horse ride, which had only happened two days earlier, as he awakened from his nap. He climbed off his feather bed and found Brenna awake and playing with her two cousins in the corner, apparently having a tea party. The three girls, however, had to follow the oldest of their quartet from the room, as he quietly walked past, shoulders back, and bearing an almost regal walk for a seven-year-old. Even his eye being swollen shut and blackened seemed to be of no import as he walked along looking like a miniature Chris Colt in his long-legged stride and confident bearing. He was their leader and their hero and must be followed at all times. He liked the role, and they liked following him around, although none of these girls was being raised to follow any man unless it was totally of their own choosing.

The four walked out onto the back porch and Joseph gave his mother a kiss and a hug. His mother, he felt, was the most beautiful woman in the whole world. His pa always telling her the same reaffirmed it even more. Shirley was the real hero to Brenna, though, and the young girl already had her mind made up that she would turn out just like her mother; beautiful but humble, graceful, dignified, and classy, no matter what. In emergencies and everyday living, the little girl had seen such a strength in her mother, an ability to survive crises and to always do what was right, no matter what the situation called for. Following Joseph's lead, she caressed the great lady, too.

"Did you four have a nice nap?"

"Yes," Rebecca, the oldest of Charley's daughters said. "I dreamed I was up on one of those mountains and some bad men were chasing me, but Joseph saved me, and I wasn't scared anymore."

Joseph's face turned red, and Shirley smiled softly.

There was the drum of hoofbeats, and the four children ran down the porch steps to see the freight wagons with supplies pulling up the long driveway. They were excited as their older counterparts trotted up and stopped in front of the long porch. Brenna and the other two girls ran up immediately to jump into the arms of a broadly grinning Uncle Joshua, who hugged each one and then quizzed them on their helpfulness to Shirley. After she confirmed their claims of being hard workers, he pulled out a licorice whip for each of them and Joseph.

Joseph was just as excited but he hid that and tried to look manly as he shook hands with his black uncle and said, "Thank you, Uncle Josh."

It was very important to Joseph to have Joshua's respect, because Joseph had so much respect for his uncle. He was so afraid when Joshua was recovering, for months, from numerous gunshot wounds after sacrificing himself to save the woman he loved. Besides his pa, Joshua was Joseph's biggest hero.

Joseph went up to his Aunt Charley and hugged her. He could feel his heart pounding in his chest when she touched him, she was so beautiful. If he felt his ma was the most beautiful creature in the world, Charley Colt Adams ran a close second.

Chris had not come forward yet, as he was getting something from Tex Westchester out of the back of the wagon. It was large, but Joseph couldn't make out what it was. Chris set it on the ground behind the wagon, and Tex sort of stood there grinning and protecting the item. Chris Colt gave his smiling wife a big hug and long kiss, which brought a giggle from the children. Chris and Shirley exchanged whispers for several seconds, then walked back to the wagon.

Standing there at the back of the wagon, one arm around Shirley, Chris Colt picked up the item with his other hand and held it while he looked at Joseph.

He said, " I spoke to your schoolteacher, Joseph."

Joseph gulped and said, "I didn't start the fight, Pa."

Chris said, "We know that."

He let go of Shirley and walked out from behind the wagon, carrying a fancy black saddle, much like his own, with tear drop-stirrup covers, called tapaderoes, and little silver conchos all over it. Joseph's mouth dropped open as his father approached and handed the saddle to him.

Chris said simply, "A man that rides a good horse ought to have a good saddle for it. C'mon, Tex, let's get these wagons unloaded."

Joseph Colt had tears in his eyes as he looked down at his new saddle. As he looked up at his pa, then his ma, he noticed a glistening in her eyes, too. Joseph dropped the saddle and ran up and grabbed his father's legs from behind in a powerful hug.

"Thank you, Pa," he said.

Chris smiled and tousled the boy's hair. "You earned it, son. Most things good that we get out of life we earn. I still haven't figured out what good I ever did to earn the right to even know your ma much less be married to her. This saddle was from her as much as me."

Joseph ran over to Shirley and gave her a big hug and kiss also. She kissed him on the cheek, then said, "Better take it to the tackroom and get some saddle soap on it and oil it up. Remember what your pa always tells you: Take care of your equipment."

The excited boy, three little girls following, struggled to carry the saddle to the large barn, but would not consider setting it down to rest his arms. Shirley looked over at Chris, unloading the wagon, and they shared a knowing smile.

Josh hefted a keg of nails and grinned at his younger brother, "Apples don't fall far from the tree, do they, little brother?"

Chris grinned and said, "Your seeds are in those apples, too." Then he looked sidelong at Charley and said, "Yours, too."

She was ecstatic. She had been so welcomed by this loving but very tough family, and every time they spoke to her it just seemed to strengthen the relationship.

The black cowboy with the shifty eyes watched with his cohorts the gathering down below at the Coyote Run Ranch from the dark timber on Spread Eagle Mountain. They had been watching the ranch many days now and keeping an eye on the inhabitants. Chris Colt had a repute that usually put his name in the same conversations with the names of people like the Earps, Bat Masterson, Doc Holliday, the Sacketts, Clay Allison, and Wild Bill Hickok. Their plan was bold and daring, and they knew they had to be extremely careful to pull it off just right.

Leaving one guard, the rest mounted up and rode back up through the trees to their camp. It had been selected carefully, near a series of beaver ponds in thick, tall timber which would dissipate the smoke from their cooking fire, and the light would not be visible to anybody in the Wet Mountain Valley down below.

The leader, Aramus Randall, had wanted posters on him hanging in many locations in Texas and Kansas. Various rewards were offered for his death or capture for kidnapping, rape, and robbery.

He was the brains of the outfit, which included one more black cowboy, a former Arikara scout-turned-cowboy, and two white cowboys. The other black cowboy was named Buck Fuller and had been a young boy accompanying his father, a fellow slave of Aramus when they killed two whites and escaped from the southern Georgia plantation where they had spent so many years. After her father's death, Buck fell in with Aramus and simply followed whatever the man said or did. Buck was quiet and nobody really understood him. The fact of the matter was that he was fairly simpleminded and Aramus doing his thinking for him and controlling his life made it easier to get by.

The Arikara scout, Johnny Shouts-at-the-Sky, had developed a bad habit in opium dens along the railroad lines. He also had developed a taste for white man's whiskey. Nobody wanted to be within Sharps distance of him then.

The two white men were first cousins, Phineas and The Second Too-Tall Clarke. There was a Too-Tall Clarke out in California and Oregon but was no relation to the Second Too-Tall, and folks referred to him as Too-Tall the First, because he was much older. The one thing the two Clarkes, who had never met, did share was a fast draw and a love for killing people, plus a real lust for gold, whiskey, and women, in that order. Phineas was the meaner of the two, and both had a wicked quick draw. Both were also very big men, not just in height but breadth as well. To date, there had not been a log across either of their trails that was ever too heavy for one or the other to lift out of the way. In any gathering, either one of the Clarkes was usually looking down at the top of every other man's head.

Aramus had the quickest draw of the gang, but he was noted for his ability with a knife. He always had a number, either hidden or exposed, open in either hand. Everyone he had killed so far had been with a knife, although two he'd wounded in gunfights and then finished them off by slitting their throats.

One more of their gang was in Westcliffe and would be joining them when he had news that Chris Colt would be gone on one of his trips. The federal marshal had been the greatest chief of scouts for the cavalry in the frontier, and they did not want him working out a trail less than a week old. The men figured that even Chris Colt couldn't unravel a well-planned and well-covered trail that old. The other gang member, a short but very stocky and barrel-chested man, was named Chink Church. He was half Chinese and half white, the offspring of a railroad camp whore and who knows which customer. Chink hated everybody and just liked to bring fear and misery into the lives of others. He had been drinking steadily in Westcliffe and trying to keep his promise not to get into any fights or get thrown in jail. There would be big money in this for him and the others, who he planned to kill off anyway for their shares, but first he needed them to pull this off. Ironically, this was the same plan of Aramus, who had already decided he would probably let Buck Fuller live, but no one else.

Chris lay on his feather bed, staring up at the ceiling in the darkness. He was leaving at daybreak with his brother and sister, but he just could not sleep. He turned his head and looked at the face of his wife, and he smiled softly. Suddenly, her steady breathing stopped and a smile appeared on her face. She turned her head, opening her eyes, and stared into his. Colt shook his head.

He said, "If one of the kids gets sick, you wake up. If something's on my mind, you wake up. Why is that?"

Shirley grinned. "It's my job."

She rubbed his chest, saying, "What is on your mind?"

Colt said, "It's silly."

Shirley said, "Not if it's keeping you awake. What's wrong, honey?"

Colt said, "I just thought about Joseph's incident with the bullies. It made me start wondering. We try very hard to be good neighbors, members of the church, our community. You know my reputation with guns and so on. Why do people always want to come after us? I just don't understand it."

Shirley thought for a minute and looked at the wall.

Finally, she spoke. "I think, when you are really good to people, I mean overly nice, that some mistake that for weakness. With others, I think some look at us and see wealth and success and want to take it from us by force."

Colt said, "Makes sense."

Shirley went on. "With many, I believe it's just stupidity. I would rather deal with an outlaw because you can prepare for them. But somebody stupid, well, you just never know what they're going to do."

Chris grinned. "You think that's a lot of it, Shirl?"

She smiled broadly. "Chris, if I were a man, you would be the last person I would ever want to try to tangle with, unless I was trying to build my reputation as a gunfighter, or thought I was so smart I could outfox you and steal from you. Or if I was just plain stupid."

Colt got serious again and said, "Do you think it will ever end?"

Shirley said, "Nope, but I'm not complaining.

You are Chris Colt. You might as well wear a target on your buckskins. I accepted that when I married you."

Colt kissed the end of her nose while she chuckled.

He said, "Maybe I'll keep you around, lady."

She gave Chris a queer look and a shiver ran up and down his spine. He pulled her into his arms and kissed her.

Four days had passed since Joseph received the new saddle. He went riding with Brenna behind him, while Rebecca and Emily rode together on a little black mare named Tillie. Many times, Shirley rode behind them in the distance, unseen. They did go fishing in Texas Creek about a mile below the house, but it was really an excuse for Joseph to ride in his new saddle again.

So Shirley was alone when the gang rode up to the Colt ranch house. Tex Westchester spotted the horses from a distance, but he was off moving one of the herds of brood mares and foals to a fresh pasture.

Chink had come in with the news that Colt, his sister, and brother were all going to Denver for several days and they knew they would have to strike now. Colt's deputy and friend, Man

Killer, had reportedly been thrown, breaking a young Appaloosa stud from his herd and was laid up in bed with a mild concussion.

The plan was simple. Everyone knew that the Colts were a very tight-knit family, and they had thousands of head of prime horseflesh as well as cattle, land holdings, and other investments. They would kidnap the children of Chris and Charley Colt and charge a handsome ransom to return the tykes unharmed. If Colt pursued or trailed them in any way, they would send him first some locks of hair, then fingers, then a child's body, until the lawman knew they meant business.

They also knew about Chris Colt's giant timber wolf pet named Kuli. A large piece of red meat soaked in laudanum would take care of that problem. The canine would sleep for hours. Shirley had also been under the weather a bit, however she was baking pies for an elderly neighbor. As they approached the ranch house and tied up, they all wore bandannas over their faces. They burst into the house and held a gun to her head when she awakened with a start.

Aramus said. "All right, Mrs. Colt, ya ain't gonna git hurt, ef'n ya do what you is tole. Ya understan' me?"

She said, "What do you want?"

Aramus said, "Jest yore children an' their cousins. We's gwine a borry 'em fer a few days until ya'll kin come up with enough money to pay ta git 'em back."

Shirley felt a surge of panic, but she fought it back. She knew that no matter what, she would never let her children or Charley's be kidnapped, especially by the looks of this gang. Yet she had to think of a plan.

Aramus said, "Mrs. Colt, pour us some coffee an' don't even think bouts pourin' it on any of us, or I'll gut ya where ya stand."

She poured coffee all the way around. She kept looking out the door for Kuli, and Aramus finally noticed her looking for him.

He said, "Forgets the wolf. He's takin' a nap."

Tex Westchester had finished up and was riding for the house when he was spotted by Chink. "The old man is riding this way fast. I can take him out of the saddle from here."

Tex was soon leading his horse past the nearby pole corral, toward the sprawling ranch house. As he came through the yard Chink and Phineas both blasted at the same time, each one shooting the horse in the upper thighs simultaneously. Tex went down with a moan on the sprawling horse, and hit facefirst as if he had been struck full-force by a railroad tie. The gang members were on him instantly, pulling him up and tying him in a chair.

Aramus smacked Chink across the face because he was closer and yelled, "Fools! Ef'n the boy heard thet, he'll light out with them girls. No more damned gunplay."

A razor-sharp bowie appeared in his hand from a sheath down his back. He held this up to Shirley's stomach and said, "When the kids come back here, don't try ta warn 'em, or I'll carve ya like a Christmas turkey."

Shirley brushed the knife to the side and went to Tex, saying, "I have to tend to him. He's hurt."

Aramus backhanded her across the face. "Ya don't do nothin' lest I tell ya. Now sit."

Tex was white-faced, but he hadn't gotten so old by being dumb. He was in severe pain, so he concentrated on keeping relaxed and unmoving so he would get his wind back. He stayed still and tried to think. What did these crooks want? he wondered.

After ten minutes, they heard the far-off giggle of a child. This was followed shortly by clearer sounds of the children talking and giggling. Shirley began to panic. Her eyes searched the room for a way out. Nobody was going to kidnap her children or her nieces. The kids were pulling up to the corral and starting to dismount when Shirley dashed for the door. Chink tried to grab her, but she sent him reeling over the kitchen table with a clatter and crash of coffee cups.

Taken by surprise, Aramus ran out the door behind her. She yelled, "Joseph, save the girls! Run! Don't stop, no mat—"

Just then the bowie knife plunged into her lower back. She stiffened with paralyzing pain.

Joseph, seeing this, screamed, "Ma!"

As he started to dismount, Shirley forced herself to spin around and grab Aramus in a bear hug.

She screamed, "No! Save the girls! Run, Joseph!"

The knife plunged into her abdomen all the way to the hilt and twisted inside her body. She screamed in agony, but refused to let go. It was pulled out and plunged in again, but she held on to her attacker with a death grip. Then she bit down on his cheek and would not let go. He stabbed her over and over, and as the life drained from her, she saw the two horses with the four children heading across the fields toward the nearby range of mountains. Joseph knew he had to save his sister and cousins.

Tex Westchester rose to his feet, chair and all,

and dived out the door. He rammed his head into the side of Aramus Randall, who was now screaming in pain himself. The old man and the outlaw went over the porch railing and into the flower bed, with half of Aramus's cheek clenched firmly between Shirley Colt's teeth. So tight was her death grip on him that two of her fingernails were caught in his shirt and ripped out when he went over the railing.

She slumped to the porch and looked up at the snow-capped peaks and smiled.

As Tex remained on the ground, moaning, Aramus struggled back up onto the porch. Pushing his kerchief against his bloody face, he said, "Yer almost dead and yer smilin'. Why?"

Weakly, she said, "I'm going to Heaven, but Chris will send you all to Hell."

Too-Tall said, "The hell you say," and drew his gun.

He pointed it at Shirley's face and cocked it. Just before he fired, she used up the last of her strength to spit at him.

Aramus poured water on Tex to rouse him and said, "Ah'm gonna let ya live, old man, so ya kin give Colt a message. Tell him, Ah got his kids and I'll kill 'em off one by one ef'n he follers. We want one million dollars in cash, and his word he ain'ta ever gonna foller us ef'n we return the young uns unhurt. I'll contact him 'bout payin the ransom."

The gang saddled up and took off after the children.

Lying among Shirley Colt's roses, carnations, and pansies, Tex could see her limp hand, fingernails missing, hanging over the edge of the porch. He turned his head and saw the children as they disappeared into the trees at the base of Spread Eagle Mountain. If any kid in the world could outwit a gang of outlaws, it would be the son of Chris Colt.

Tex tried to stand but couldn't He rolled over on his back and looked up at the sky. He whispered, "God, ya may not recognize me. We ain't palavered much, but this here woman is the finest I ever knowed in all mah born days. Please take her up there with ya, an' let her know Colt'll be joinin' her someday. Treat her good. She deserves it, sir. Please help them young uns ta git away. One last thing. Ya kin let me go under, but first let me git somewhere's where I kin git a holt a Colt so's he kin hunt down and kill them murderin' bastards."

Tex dragged his old body forward toward the corral. He made it to his horse and inched the horse over until he was in front of the watering trough. Holding the saddle horn as tightly as possible, Tex yelled, "Hiya!" and gritted his teeth.

The horse took off at an immediate gallop and, launching himself off of the trough with considerable pain, he was able to swing up and over the saddle. Tex galloped by the porch and the bloody, lifeless body of Shirley Colt. He choked back his tears, knowing he was now on a life-and-death mission to save four little children, and he needed all his wits. He dashed out the driveway and turned the horse for the ten-mile run south to Westcliffe.

After two miles, Tex reined up, feeling himself getting light-headed. He took his lariat and ran it over himself and under the horse's neck and belly several times and tied himself to the animal so he wouldn't pass out and fall off. The horse seemed to sense his desperation and moved easily under his master's hand.

Soon he arrived at the next ranch to the south, belonging to his friend, Soft Hardtack Oldham. Soft was standing outside his ranch house, a Spencer rifle tucked under a sinewy left arm. Seeing the horse, Soft laid the rifle against the hitch post and ran to his friend's side.

"Mary Catherine," the old man yelled in a thick Carolina accent, "git out heah quick an' bring towels! Heah?"

A pleasant-looking woman in her early sixties ran out the door seconds later and drawled, "I Swanee!"

Despite her shock, she immediately went to work on the old man's wounds, even before Soft could get him off the horse.

On the ground, Tex said, "Forgit me! Soft, old pard, ya gotta fork yer fastest mustang and git the hell ta Westcliffe. Ya gotta send a tellygraph ta the sherrif up in Denver and tell 'em ta find Chris Colt and git him back here quick. The hombres that bushwhacked me kilt poor ole Shirley Colt, God rest her soul, an' they taken out after the young uns, Colt's and Charlotte's both. They going ta kidnap them and claim a million dollars from old Chris."

As Soft ran to his barn to get a bronc, Tex said sadly, "Ya know what thet young woman done, Mary Catherine? You know what she done?"

Mary Catherine, starting to cry, said, "Now, Tex, hush up."

"I gotta tell you this. Thet beautiful young lady, Shirley Colt, held on ta the leader a the yahoos and would not let go whist he stabbed her over and over. Ya known why? So the young uns could make a getaway. She knew she would die. She knew she was a goner, but she would not let go and then she ups and takes a chunk outta his cheek on top of it all. Thet there was the saltiest, purtiest, toughest, and best woman I ever knowed in all mah born days."

Mary Catherine had to stop and bury her face in her gingham skirt while she sobbed openly.

Soft came out of the barn at a canter on a wiry mouse-colored half Morgan, half mustang.

He slid to a stop by Tex and said, "Woman, kin ya'll hitch up the wagon and git him inta that doc in Westcliffe by yerself?"

She said, "Git out of here, and don't spare the horse. We're fine!"

Tex said, "Soft, tell the sheriff thet the kids headed up Spread Eagle Mountain and the yahoos warn't fur behind. I dint see Kuli nowhars. Mebbe they kilt him, but I bet he could lead the sheriff ta them ef'n he could git him ta obey."

Kuli was Chris Colt's pet almost-two-hundred-pound wolf.

Soft nodded, gave his wife a wink, and put the spurs to his horse. He dashed down the driveway, and Mary Catherine looked down at Tex and wiped a tear off his cheek.

"He's a good man," Tex said.

She smiled. "Once he quit that drinking. He never knew about us, you know. I think he might have suspected it a time or two, but he has never asked."

Tex said, "Good, 'cause thet was years ago, Mary Catherine. You two was split up, and I din't know him then. Now, it don't matter no more. You made the right choice, old girl. Like Ah said, he's a good man."

She smiled and said, "You're right, Tex, but isn't it amazing how we ended up here in this little place so many miles from Texas. How do you suppose that happened?"

Tex said, "Coinceedence. It ain't no big miracle, Mary Catherine. People are makin' fortunes overnight heah. Gold mines, silver mines. Everyone with some sand heads this way or passes through. Yer old man gots sand, and ya need to 'member thet always."

She looked after Soft down the darkened driveway, imagining him off in the night, pushing his horse. She smiled softly.

"Tex, you're very right, you know," she said, "I am a lucky woman, but you would have been a great catch, too, for any woman."

"Naw, ain't likely," Tex mused, "I got me a past, too. I always look at mah backtrail, waitin' for a certain star-packer ta show up. Ah know he ain't a gonna, but I always em lookin' over mah shoulder anyhows."

She said, "I know about the shooting in Texas. Was she very beautiful?"

Tex cleared his throat, saying, "Like the sun when it comes up over the mountains of a early mornin'. Ya know when ya look out at the dew on the grass in the meadows then. And ya see them purty purple and yeller floweer sprinkled all through the grass?"

She nodded.

He went on. "Wal, thet feelin' ya git when ya see thet was what I was juest talkin' about. Thet's how she used ta make me feel every time Ah looked at 'er."

Mary Catherine smiled, "Well, Tex Westchester, you are a poet."

Tex said, "Wal, Ah preciate ya tryin' ta taken mah mind off'n what jest happened, Girlie, but it ain'ta gonna work. Ah gotta git mahself up and round, so's ah kin help Chris Colt when he get's here."

She said, "Tex, let's get you into the house. There's no way you're going to make it back out on your feet by then, though."

Tex said, "The hell, you say."

CHAPTER 4

Hell Hath No Fury
Like a Colt Wronged

Tex was moving slow but doing all he could to
hide it when Chris, Joshua, and Charlotte Colt
rode up the driveway and into the barn. They
immediately unsaddled and rubbed down their
horses, giving each one oats, and forking some
hay to them in their individual stalls. Tex waited
for them to emerge from the barn's large doorway. The word had already spread up and down
the Wet Mountain Valley, the Arkansas Valley,
and the southern Front Range. No sooner had the
trio entered the barn than numerous wagons and
horses loaded with friends of the Colt family
started coming down the driveway and pulling
up behind the big ranch house. Men and women
came forward, most bearing baskets of food, and
started offering condolences.

Chris, Joshua, and Charley emerged from the barn, travel-weary and worn from the quick journey back from Denver. Tex struggled forward with his cane and met them. He was still in terrific pain. He walked directly up to Chris and looked as if he were about to cry.

Tex said, "Chris, Ah tell ya. Ah did everything Ah could ta stop it."

Colt patted him on the shoulder and said, "You don't have to explain that."

Tex went on, "Colt, thet woman a yours. She held thet man whislt he stabbed her over and over jest so's the young uns could git a runnin' head start. Yer boy taken charge a them children and got them the hell outta here. He's yer son, sir, and they's gonna play hobs catchin' up ta him, I jest know it."

Charlotte came forward and took Tex in her arms and started crying. Joshua put his arm around Chris's big shoulders, and they walked into the big house. The undertaker had her laid out in a coffin packed in ice, which was covered by a flowered quilt. As Chris looked down at his wife, a whimper escaped his lips. He hardly noticed all the men and women who came up offering condolences and patting him on the back.

Chris put his arm around Joshua's shoulder

and led him away from everyone. There was now a very grim look on his face, but tears remained in his eyes.

Chris whispered, "You need to bury Shirley for me, brother. I have this thing to do."

Joshua soberly responded, "I know, Chris. You go. Save the children. I'll be here, and Shirley." Joshua choked up but went on. "Shirl will be with God. She's there now."

All eyes followed Chris as he ran up the stairs. Charley fell across Shirley's body and cried while others tried to comfort her. Soon, Charlotte stood up, dried her tears, and looked around. She took Joshua by the arm and walked him across the room, while he hugged her tightly.

She started to speak, but he cut her off. "I know. They're your little girls. I'll take care of everything here."

She grabbed her older brother's head and pulled it down, kissing him on the cheek. Then she tore up the stairs and knocked on Chris's door.

There was no answer, so Charley said, "Chris?"

The door opened, and she saw a bedroll and saddlebags on his bed. Chris was holding a leather bag into which he was pouring .45 bullets.

She said, "We have to talk to Tex and get the details."

Colt said, "What do you mean 'we'?"

She said, "They're after my children, too."

Colt said, "I'll get them all back."

Charley said, "I know. I'll be with you. Don't even discuss it, Christopher. I'm going with you. Shirley is also my family, and so are Joseph and Brenna."

Chris Colt stared at his younger sister, and she stared back. Finally he looked away. "Get the story from Tex while you're packing."

Charley went to the door and said, "If they think they're going to harm our children, they're going to learn that they're dealing with us, and some blazing Colts."

She disappeared into the hallway and closed the door. The mighty Chris Colt immediately fell across the bed and cried long and hard, racking sobs.

Between sobs, Colt said, "Oh God, how I loved you!"

There was a great deal of murmuring in the large living room of the main Colt house when Charley entered, wearing buckskins head to toe and wearing a pair of Colt Navy .36's tied down in quick-draw holsters. She also wore a Smith & Wesson Pocket .32 tucked into her gun belt in front. All the murmurs were silenced, though, when Chris Colt appeared at the top of the stairway. He came down the stairs, not looking left or right, up or down. He carried his bedroll with a Cheyenne bow and quiver of arrows wrapped up in it. Colt wore fringed buckskin trousers and jackets as well, along with his matched Colt Peacemakers with the hand-carved pearl handles, as well as his antler-handled, beaded bowie knife. Chris Colt's large-roweled Mexican spurs jingled loudly as the little bells on the side swung back and forth. Dark black-and-bright red war paint was slashed all over his handsome face. Most of the lower half of his face was painted black, and the upper part had streaks of red gravitating outward from the center.

Beaded saddlebags over his shoulder, along with the bedroll and a Winchester carbine in his right hand, Chris Colt walked into the kitchen followed by Charley. Joshua blocked well-meaning onlookers from following. Chris poured Charley a cup of coffee, and the two quickly packed food into their bags. Joshua walked into the kitchen, followed by the Custer County sheriff, who tried to speak but choked on his words. Chris didn't speak either. He just removed his badge and tossed it to the sheriff. Colt shook with Joshua, and Charley hugged the oldest brother.

Chris said to Joshua, "Bury my wife?"

Joshua said, "You go do what must be done. I'll handle everything here."

Chris nodded and walked out the door. Charley caught up to him as he crossed the yard. Tex was barely able to move but still hobbled up to the pair on his crutches and Colt put a hand on the oldster's shoulder.

Colt said, "I know that you did everything you possibly could, Tex."

Tex got choked up again and said, "Colt, when ya ketch up with them sidewinders, ya kill 'em, ya heah?"

Chris looked grimly at the ranch hand and patted him on the head. He entered the barn. When he and Charley came out, leading their horses, Colt was greeted by the sight of Man Killer, his deputy and longtime sidekick. The handsome young Nez Percé rancher was being helped out of the back of a buckboard by his wife, Jennifer Banta. Man Killer had his head bound. He came toward Colt. Man Killer started to speak but stopped and Colt gave him a nod of understanding. A single tear ran down Man Killer's right cheek. He motioned Colt over as he reached inside his shirt. Man Killer pulled out a small pouch, which was hanging around his neck on a leather cord. He placed it over Colt's neck and the big man tucked it into his own buckskin shirt. It was Man Killer's medicine pouch, which carried personal mementos which were very important. It was to give him more spiritual power and keep him protected at all times. Colt reached out a hand and patted Man Killer once on the cheek and mounted, turned his horse, squeezed its ribs, and rode off toward the nearby towering mountains, with Charley following close behind.

Man Killer noticed something as they rode off across the pastures and mentioned it to Joshua and Tex, "Look at War Bonnet's tail."

The two men looked at the fleet-footed black-and-white paint and both noticed that his long flowing tail had been tied into a big overhand knot.

Joshua said, "You mean the knot in his tail?"

Man Killer said, "When a brave goes into war, he ties his horse's tail in a knot. Your brother goes off to war."

Tex said, "Wal, them buzzards better bring theyselves a damned army if they want a stand a chance against Colt, and thet little sister a his, too. She durned shore has yer Colt blood in her veins, Joshua."

Brother and sister got their horses, and set off riding. Getting close to the tree line at the base of the mountain, Chris had second thoughts. "Maybe you should go back and let me handle this."

Charlotte said, "Chris, the subject is closed. Two of those children are mine, and Shirley was also my best friend besides being my sister-in-law."

Colt said, "I won't broach the subject again."

"Thank you, and I want you to know that I will be there to help you. You won't have to worry about me getting hurt," replied Charley.

"We have a worse problem to worry about."

Charlotte started to ask, "What?" when large snowflakes started swirling down to the ground. "This is not a problem, Chris. This is a blessing."

"Why?" he asked.

"Because it will help cover the children's trail so the outlaws cannot locate them," Charley explained.

"But, Charley, we won't be able to either."

Charley beamed. "Excuse me, sir, but are you not the mighty Chris Colt? You will find the trail even when others cannot."

"How do you know?"

"Because you are my brother, and you—we will not give up. Do you understand?"

Chris felt embarrassed. "You're right. I was a chief of scouts for the U.S. Cavalry for a long time. They must have felt I could unwind a trail, huh?"

"Exactly," she replied.

Chris said, "We better get up in those trees and find a camping spot or we are not going to trail anybody."

With that, he said, "Canter." He squeezed War Bonnet's ribs, and the big paint tore across the meadow, with Charley in hot pursuit.

It was the middle of the night when Joseph awakened with a start and looked around, trying to figure out where he was. The fire had gone down, so he fed some logs into it. It blazed up, the flames and shadows dancing on the walls of the cave. All three girls were sleeping soundly. The cave offered plenty of protection from the howling wind and the late-summer blizzard swirling around outside.

The natural cave was just above the timberline. He had found it when fishing at Lakes of the Clouds one time with his pa and Man Killer. As much as his mother had worried about him,

Chris liked it when his son wandered off in the wilderness to explore on his own. Chris Colt learned a lot of his parenting by watching nature and imitating what seemed to work. He believed in the occasional spanking to teach a lesson, because he'd seen a she bear spank a cub to get it up a tree if danger was near. He also knew that bears, lions, and other creatures let their offspring wander a little when they were old enough, so the youngster could start developing savvy which would keep it alive as it grew older.

During one of those excursions young Colt had found the natural cave and explored it. It was actually a large cavern formed by big boulders which fell in just the right configuration, but it now kept the children and the two horses, Spot and Tillie, hidden away and sheltered from the storm. The children had even picked large bunches of meadow grasses for the horses to feed on in the cave.

Meanwhile, the killers were only a few thousand feet directly below the children, huddled in an aspen grove with a large fire going. They had to take turns staying awake to keep the fire going, not realizing that the large fire was boiling them on one side, but they were freezing on the other.

*   *   *

Less than two miles to the south, Charley and Chris Colt lay in their bedrolls on either side of a small fire, with flat rocks set up on three sides to reflect the heat toward them. The camp was hidden away in a small, heavily wooded bowl with a small glacial creek running past. Chris had pulled tall evergreen saplings over and made a roof to keep them and their horses relatively shielded from the blizzard.

Lying there, Chris pictured the woman he had loved more than life itself sacrificing herself, taking a knife into her body over and over to save the children. He felt such guilt because he had not been there to protect her. Colt could not keep back the tears and he tried to keep Charley from hearing him, but she could see his big back convulsing as he silently cried.

Chris stiffened as he felt a pair of hands grab him gently.

Charley said, "Go ahead, brother. It's just you and me here. Every man needs to cry sometime."

Chris Colt, the bigger-than-life legendary fighter, rolled over and looked up into the eyes of his beautiful sister, tears clouding his own. She stroked his hair gently, and Colt dropped his head on her lap and wrapped his big arms around her waist. Then the dam burst. He cried harder than he ever had in his life. Charlotte cried, too, but quietly, and more out of sympathy for her newfound brother. Also, because she now had a brother, two of them actually, that she could share feelings with unashamed.

After Colt stopped crying, they both sat by the fire and drank coffee, talking long into the night.

Chris explained, "This blizzard is bad, but in the Colorado mountains, chances are the snow will all be melted away by late afternoon tomorrow. In fact, it will probably be hot as the dickens tomorrow. We won't take out after them right after daybreak. I want the snow to melt so we can pick up some good sign on the trail."

Charley said, "Won't this blizzard obliterate all tracks?"

Colt said, "No, if it was rain it would. Actually, the powdery snow probably won't affect the tracks at all. Besides, if the children haven't been caught yet, Joseph will probably try to leave me some kind of sign."

Charlotte said, "But what about trying to find the children before they freeze?"

Chris replied, "I can only hope that Joseph paid attention to all the teaching I did when we were out in the mountains. He's young but the boy is smart, and he's got sand."

"His name is Colt, isn't it?" Charlotte said.

Chris sadly replied, "It didn't help Shirley much to marry a Colt."

Charlotte said, "Look, you probably are feeling horrible guilt right now, thinking you didn't protect her."

Colt hanged his head saying, "That's putting it mildly."

Charley continued, "But you don't understand. Shirley told me that she could have married some banker, merchant, or rancher and maybe have a less dangerous life, but that is not what she wanted. I talked with Tex, and he said that Shirley could have cooperated, but she didn't want the children taken so she chose not to. She knew that they would kill her but did it anyway to protect the children. It was Shirley's decision, not your inability to protect her, Chris. And it was the insane act of some animals who have no right to call themselves men. You cannot blame yourself or it will kill you."

Colt lit a cigarillo and blew the smoke toward the fire.

He pondered her words a minute and finally said, "Maybe you're right, Charlotte, but I'll tell you one thing right now. I will never marry again. Never."

Charlotte said, "Chris, you just lost your wife. Of course you feel that way."

"No," Colt said. "I will never marry again. I have given my word."

That closed the subject right there. Charley knew any further talk would be futile.

"Where do you suppose the children are?"

Colt said, "Somewhere warm, I hope."

Joseph walked outside the cave and looked at the swirling snow. For the first time since the snow had begun he felt some cold. The young boy urinated and shook his shoulders and back as a chill racked his small body. Would he get his sister and cousins out of this situation until his pa could arrive and save them? he wondered. He steeled himself, thinking, I am the son of Chris Colt. I am going to keep us alive and safe. I'm not going to act and think like a little boy. I'm going to think and act like my pa would. Joseph looked into the darkness and the blowing flakes and wondered where the outlaws were. He was very glad that the snow started because he knew his father could locate him and the snow would hide his tracks from the killers.

Joseph felt a shiver as he stared at the swirling flakes and some words echoed in his mind. "Joseph, button your coat." The words were his mother's, and he subconsciously reached down below his chin and buttoned the top button on his coat. Just that movement brought a flood of realization into his mind, and Joseph ran forward into the storm, crying.

He looked up into the white churning abyss of blowing, twisting crystalline shapes and cried out, "God! God! Please bring my mommy back! Please? I don't want her to die!"

He stood there, flakes falling down on his face, the coldness of their touch on his cheeks and eyelids, bringing him to the cold realization that this was not to be. He fell down on his knees and bent over, crying hard. This went on for several minutes and turned into sniffles, and finally an occasional convulsion of his diaphragm muscles.

He then rose, wiped his face, and now with a serious and tough look on his young face, he stared out into the darkness and said quietly, "Please, Pa, come and save us."

Joseph threw his shoulders back and quietly returned to the fire, warming himself.

Buck Fuller shivered almost uncontrollably as he got out of his bedroll and went over to the fire. He threw more logs on, and the flames leapt into the sky. Their silhouettes danced on the aspen canopy above. Buck kicked Phineas Clarke in the ribs. Phineas was supposed to be tending the fire and standing watch.

Phineas jumped up cursing and grabbed for his gun. He stopped when he heard a loud clicking noise. It was the hammer of a .44 being eared back. Both he and Buck froze and looked at Aramus, who was holding the gun on Phineas. The others started stirring.

Buck said, "He let the fire die down. He was snorin' like a old granpaw."

"You puts dat gun away now," Aramus warned.

Phineas complied, but explained, "Thet sumbitch come up and kicked me in the ribs whilst was jest restin' mah eyes. Ah was watchin' the fahr. They warn't nothin' wrong with it."

Aramus put his gun away and said, "Hush. We got Chris Colt trailin' us, you fools."

Too-Tall said, "He ain't gonna foller us. We left a strong warnin'."

Aramus said, "You has yo haid up so high in the sky they couldn't reach up ta put brains in there. We kilt his old lady, fool."

Chink Church said, "Why don't we just wait and bushwhack Colt after the storm clears out?"

Aramus said, "You want to try to ambush Chris Colt?"

Chink said, "Hell yeah, I'll do it. He's just a man. He runs his water just like I do."

Aramus grinned, saying, "Lots of men is livin' in Boot Hill right now what had de same way a thinkin.' "

Chink said, "Like I said. I'll wait here when you all go and take care of Chris Colt."

Aramus said, "How we get de bounty then?"

Chink said, "Joshua Colt and that sister of theirs. They'll pay."

Aramus didn't like challenges from his men and especially not from Chink. He was dangerous.

The leader said, "Shore, help yoself."

Johnny Shouts-at-the-Sky hadn't spoken, but now he said softly, "I think we have made a mistake. We should go home, each man alone."

"Wal, ef your scared, Johnny," Aramus said.

Johnny said, "I stay, fight any man, but we make bad medicine. We will die."

"Speak for yourself, Johnny," Chink said, "I'm gonna kill Chris Colt and that will take care of our problems."

Johnny smiled sourly and said, "You will die first."

Chink gave the half-breed a dirty look, but something inside him suddenly turned cold. He felt a lump in his throat and tried to swallow, but he felt as if he had swallowed a warmed-up lump of hard cotton.

The Second Too-Tall Clarke meekly said, "Ya know, Johnny might be right. Mebbe we bit off a chunk a jerky what'll be hard to swagger. I figgered we was jest gonna git in theah, grab the young uns, leave us a ransom note, and git out. Now we're gonna have the toughest man in the country ready to take all a our hair 'cause we kilt his woman. Mebbe we ought a cut an' run."

Aramus angrily replied, "Mebbe ya ain't got no hair, Too-Tall. Is that yo problem, boy?"

Too-Tall felt humiliated. "Naw. It's jest all those stories I heerd about Chris Colt. His first wife was a Sioux, and she and his kid got kilt by some Crows. Colt hunts 'em all down and kills 'em one by one with a knife. I heard he scalped and cut up every one of 'em, too."

Chink said sarcastically, "Yep, Wyatt Earp stands seven foot tall, too."

Aramus said, "Let's git some sleep. We's got some young uns ta blast tomorrow."

Too-Tall said, "What do ya mean, blast?"

Aramus said, "Ah done tole you, boy. Colt is after our hides now. We kilt his woman. We's might as well kill the young uns when we gets 'em. He can only try ta kill us once."

Too-Tall said, "This is too much fer me. I'm pullin' mah freight."

Aramus drew his gun again and cocked it, with an angry sneer on his face. "Mebbe you boys is so worried bout Colt's rep, ya done forgot bouts mine. Ya ever heerd what I done wif a knife, or a gun?"

Too-Tall cleared his throat but did not speak. He realized he had stepped across a line and was in serious trouble.

Aramus waved his pistol around, a blazing fire almost visible in his dark brown eyes. Teeth clenched, he said, "Awright, y'all. Yo boys said ya wanted me as yo leader. Now den, when Ah says somethin' ya does it. It can't be no other way, or someone dies, dey dies hard, maybe gut-shot, maybe belly-slit. Now, who wanna leave?"

Nobody spoke or even moved, and he continued. "Now, who wanna try me for the boss job?"

Again, nobody spoke, and he continued. "Chink, you wants ta die, you can try ta bushwhack Colt. Da rest a you, we is gonna find dem kids and kill 'em. Den we go collect da ransom. Mebbe, ef'n we kin lose Colt, we'll head back down ta his ranch and tell his brother dat he's up here dead and we want a ransom now for da kids. We gets the ransom, split it up, and taken off in every direction."

He looked around, scowling at everyone. "Any questions?"

Not even a nod.

He went on, "Den let's git some shut-eye. We goes after dem in da mornin' ef da snowin' stops."

Rebecca, Emily, and Brenna all yawned simultaneously as Joseph awakened them. "Come on, get up you three," he said. "It's morning, and it's quit snowing. We have to try again to make it back home."

The three girls stirred and finally awakened fully after several minutes.

Brenna started crying suddenly and said, "Joseph, is Mommy living with God now?"

Joseph choked and started to cry but stopped himself. "Yeah, she is, but we cannot think about that now, Brenna. None of us can. We have to think about being brave and not getting caught. When Pa finds us and we're safe, then we can think about what happened. Can you be brave?"

Brenna sniffled, saying, "I can."

"Me, too," Rebecca said.

Emily followed with, "Me, too."

The three girls sat down by the fire, and Joseph handed each of them a birch bark bowl filled with stew he made by boiling water with jerky shaved into it with his knife, then adding several wild herbs and vegetables. His father had taught Joseph to always carry jerky, matches, a whetstone, hooks and fishing line, matches, and other essentials. Furthermore, Joseph wore an elk antler-handled knife on his hip everywhere he went. A gift from his Uncle Joshua, it was his pride and joy, and he kept it as sharp as his father's knife. Chris Colt constantly lectured his son on how the mountains could be your friend if respected and treated right, or how they could kill you if you didn't respect their power.

The snow storm was long gone, and the early-morning sun was already melting the snow away down in Wet Mountain Valley. Down there, the temperatures by late afternoon would probably reach up into the high seventies. This was the way things were in the Colorado Rockies and many a tenderfoot had died in these mountains because they did not understand nature's awesome power.

Up above, the snow was melting rapidly and thousands of little streams of water ran together, meshing into the many little creeks cascading and tumbling down the mountainside. It was one of these powerful little rivulets that was the undoing of the children. As they started off slowly across the wet, snowy rocks, the horses had to make a slight jump across one such stream. When they did, Mrs. Cranberry fell from Emily's little hand and was swept down the mountain. Mrs. Cranberry was a rag doll that Charley had made for her when she was still in a crib. The little girl started crying. While the others tried to calm her, Joseph looked down the stream in worry. The stream might pass right through the camp of the outlaws. Joseph picked up the pace but hoped and prayed that his father would find the doll and not the killers.

Sure enough, Johnny Shouts-at-the Sky spotted the object tumbling down the mountain stream and jumped off his horse to snatch it out of the water. He held it up for the others to see. They all grinned, turned their horses uphill, and put the spurs to them.

Chris Colt poured water on the fire and spread the sticks around. "It's melting quicker than I thought it would. Let's get after them."

Charley quickly struck camp while Colt saddled the horses. They were soon on the trail.

Within an hour they stopped, while Chris dismounted. Something shiny just off the trail had caught his eye. He walked uphill about ten feet and bent over. As he stood up, examining the object, he smiled. He turned his head back down to the trail and scoured the ground. A bigger smile crossed his face.

Chris walked over to Charley and handed her the shiny little silver tack. She gave him a questioning look.

Colt held up his hand. He went back to the other spot he had been right next to the trail and knelt down, trying to blow the remaining snow off some rocks, but it was too wet. Slowly, carefully, he swept the snow off two rocks, one atop the other on the right side of the trail.

Charlotte said, "All right, Chris, explain this."

Colt said, "That silver tack came from Joseph's new saddle Shirley and I gave him. Those tacks run all the way around the edge of the saddle. It wouldn't have come loose. He apparently pried it loose with his knife and tried to leave it where he figured I might see but maybe others wouldn't. The rocks there, see one flat one atop another flat one?"

She nodded.

He went on, "That's a trail sign we all use; Joshua, Man Killer, Tex, and me. We use flat rocks along the right side of a trail. One on top of another means turn right. Three in a row means keep going ahead. Two in a row with a tiny one on top of the first means turn left, and three rocks one on top of the other means go back." He looked up in satisfaction. "I sure am proud of that little boy, Charley."

"You and me both," she said. "Do you think that the children have still avoided capture?"

Colt said, "I'd say so. They're up high, and it looks like the outlaws have gone on south along the trail. I'll bet Joseph has tried going up high to make a signal fire the ranch could spot. Or maybe he's just trying to elude them. Let's go on a ways and check the trail some more. Then we'll come back and head uphill here. I want to find the outlaws' camp."

Charley said, "Why is that important?"

Colt said, "Well, you mentioned that I have done a bit of tracking. Their overnight campsite can tell me an awful lot about them."

Colt lit up a cigarillo and they rode on, Chris leaning off to the right, the uphill side, watching the trail. Before he finished his smoke, they were standing next to the cold fire of the outlaws' camp. Colt left War Bonnet with Charley and bade her to stay back while he crawled around the camp on hands and knees.

Chris explained the signs. "Well, one is an Indian."

Charley said, "How do you know? I didn't see any moccasin prints or unshod horse tracks."

Colt said, "One is wearing old cavalry boots and cavalry spurs. I can tell because they dig into the dirt. He walks a little pigeon-toed, probably one of the Plains tribes, maybe a former scout, and he mounts his horse from the right. He swings up without using stirrups. Indian way. He's also careful and watches the back trail a lot. He has probably tried to talk them into going higher because several times he has started uphill, but has ended up turning back downhill. I bet because he's been ordered to. Going up high is the Indian way also. Joseph remembers that, bless his little heart."

Charlotte said, "No wonder everyone is amazed by your abilities. What else can you tell?"

Chris said, "They are like most outlaws, lazy and thoughtless. They did not make a good camp last night, and their fire was too big, so they froze on one side and burned on the other. By now they are probably fighting with each other a lot and pretty miserable."

"How do you know all that?"

Colt answered, "The fire was too big, because they all turned so much in their bedrolls and slid away from the fire at times. Every one of them did it except the Indian. He stayed out away from the fire in the darkness and probably put the cold out of his mind. I also know that the fire was too big because those leaves up above their camp are all scorched. See?"

She looked up at the branches over the fire site and saw the curled and brown leaves. Charley nodded affirmatively.

Chris said, "Let's follow them a little farther and see if they still are heading south."

They mounted up and had just started out of the camp when Chris reined up again, saying, "Uh-oh."

He jumped down and started reading sign on the ground, continually looking uphill.

Charlotte said, "What's wrong, Chris?"

He replied, "Several of them jumped across this waterway, but one stopped, dismounted, knelt by the creek, and reached down. Then they all turned and headed uphill. Apparently something floated down the stream from up above, probably some kind of sign from the kids."

Charley looked alarmed. "Let's go," she said.

Colt stood up quickly—and that is what saved his life. A bullet flashed past his buttocks and whined off a rock. Charley immediately drew and fired while diving from the saddle. She got off two rounds before she hit the ground and knocked the wind out of herself, but they both heard the shooter moaning behind a rock twenty paces away along the trail.

Chris was on his belly, now aiming down his right-hand gun. The shooter's foot was sticking out from behind the rock and barely moving.

Colt said, "You okay?"

She didn't answer, and he looked at her carefully. She couldn't catch her breath.

Chris said, "Stand up behind that tree, then jump up and land on your heels with your knees locked."

She did so and was able to breathe immediately.

"Thanks," she whispered with a sigh.

He nodded and squeezed off a shot. The bushwhacker's foot flinched, and he screamed in pain, but still lay behind the rock.

"Cover me," Chris commanded.

He scrambled to his feet and ran toward the rock, gun outstretched. Charley shadowed him to the left, both of her guns drawn. Chink Church lay behind the rock, a bloody hole through his left foot and two through his chest. Colt walked up to the man.

Sternly he asked, "Which man stabbed my wife?"

The hard man spat at Chris and said, "Stick it—agh!" he screamed as Chris stepped down hard on his bloody foot.

Charley said, "Like my brother said. Who killed his wife?"

Chink nodded his head, letting them know he would talk. Colt let the pressure off his foot.

The bad man resignedly said, "Aramus Randall. He's a nigra. Big. You takin' me in ta hang now, Colt?"

Charley said, "No," and shot him between the eyes.

She stared at the corpse then looked up at Chris. Tears flooded her eyes.

Chris said, "That's the way this has to go down, Charley. It's not murder; it's self-defense. Our family has gotten too well-known, too famous. If we leave their bodies behind it will stop others with the same idea."

Charlotte said, "I know. I just always wanted to be a housewife, not a killer."

Colt said, "You're not a killer."

Charlotte said, "Yes, yes, I am. It's all right. Let's save the children." They mounted and headed up the mountain on the trail of the outlaws.

They kept climbing, stopping after fifteen hundred feet to let the horses blow. They were getting a lot closer to the timberline now.

Charley said, " I wonder where the children are."

Joseph looked down from his perch as the men approached. The other three kids were hidden with the horses up higher and across a deep basin above the timberline. It was all rock getting to them, and they were amidst a giant tumble of boulders in a deep avalanche chute. Snowslides year in and year out had grabbed the boulders and dragged them down the mountainside along with tons of snow to make a monstrous pile of rocks. Joseph knew that the other three would be safe for now, and he had left instructions with Brenna to head downhill and try to make it to the ranch if he was caught or killed.

The outlaws were getting closer to his trap. Joseph was about a hundred feet above them, hidden among some rocks. Aramus was favoring his side where Tex had crashed into him and kept touching his torn cheek every few seconds. Every ache made his anger grow.

The men were being led by Johnny, the former scout, and Joseph was excited that the cagey

Indian was reading his trail sign, apparently not suspecting that it was a fake.

The second man in line was Too-Tall Clarke. He seemed edgy, and he looked off into the dark woods to his left continuously. As he came abreast of a wide bush next to the trail, Joseph threw a large rock toward a shale slide. When it hit the shale, it cracked like a whip. As Joseph had planned, Too-Tall dived off his horse and into the thick bushes. The outlaw impaled his side and his shin on two of the sticks the boy had sharpened to a point and buried in the ground. Joseph had planted six of them about a foot apart. Too-Tall panicked as he looked at the spikes protruding from his body. Blood seeped from his wounds and he was going into shock.

The boy reveled at the screams of pain from below, knowing his little ambush plan had worked. Now it was time for phase two. The boy yanked on a lasso attached to a log holding up a rock pile he and the girls had quickly created. With the second jerk the log came loose, and the pile of rocks started down the hill toward the rest of the gang. As they tumbled almost straight down the steep slope, they gathered larger rocks, which came with them.

Aramus saw the slide first and screamed,

"Avalanche!" He put the spurs to his horse and rolled him back the way he had come.

The other gang members scattered in every direction. Buck Fuller fractured his forearm as a pumpkin-sized rock hit his horse in the right foreleg, breaking it, and the black cowboy was tossed down below onto more rocks. Aramus rode over after the slide and put a bullet through the screaming horse's head.

Buck said, "Now what's does I do?"

Aramus wheeled his horse and said, "Walk."

They all scoured the rocks up above to try to locate whoever had wreaked so much havoc, but they found nothing, except a marmot whistling much higher. Joseph had already planned an escape route, a small natural path that he could easily run along, bent over, and be hidden from view down below. The path led through a field of boulders and rocks, hiding both him and his tracks. Quickly he beat a path back toward the bowl in which his sister and cousins were hidden.

The three girls were concerned because they were hidden away from view so well, they didn't know what was going on. They could see only a very steep, rocky chute above them which was covered with snow.

Buck Fuller moaned in pain as he looked at

his arm, hanging helplessly at his side. Phineas scrambled among the rocks and handed Buck the canteen off the dead horse.

"Busted yer arm, huh?" he asked stupidly.

Buck said, "Yas, I cain't do nothin' wif dis arm."

Johnny rode up and started making a splint for Buck's arm, while Phineas stripped the saddle and tack from the dead horse's body.

An hour later, with Too-Tall bandaged up and swaying in the saddle and Buck Fuller walking in the rear, the outlaws took off again after what they had thought were helpless little youngsters.

Phineas said, "Where do you suppose Colt is? We haven't seen or heard anything since we heard the shots down the mountain."

Aramus said, "Whey is Colt? Who does ya think just bushwhacked us? You doesn't think it was some snot-nosed young uns, do ya? Thet was Colt what bushwhacked us, and we better keep a close eye ta the backtrail."

Phineas said, "I don't know, Aramus. We shore bit off a tough hunk a horsemeat here. Why don't we pack it in?"

Aramus didn't respond. He just wheeled his horse and headed uphill.

Johnny was already ahead of the group, and as Aramus approached him, the outlaw leader said, "Ef'n ya was gittin away from us from up dere, an' ya doesn't wants ta be follered, which is da only way ta go?"

"Over rocks. Up to big valley above trees," Johnny replied.

Aramus said, "You're right. Let's git 'im."

Fifteen minutes later, Johnny found a track of Joseph's where he'd slipped off a rock and stepped into mud between two rocks. Johnny yelled to the others, "It was not the mighty Colt! It was his boy!"

"Sumbitch!" Phineas exclaimed. "His little brat done all that to us, and we ain't even had ta deal with Colt yet. I tell ya, Aramus, we're in the wrong game."

Enraged, Aramus turned and fired. Phineas screamed as he grabbed his hand. Blood ran between his fingers, as the web of his hand started burning where Aramus had notched it. Aramus never spoke a word. He just turned around in the saddle and rode toward Johnny. Phineas's anger started churning inside him, and his other hand went down to the handle of his .44.

As if he had eyes in the back of his head, Aramus calmly said, "Phineas, ya kin try a back-shot, ef'n ya think ya kin git aways wif it."

Phineas's hand immediately moved away from the gun. He felt a burning sensation in his throat as bile came up from his stomach. He looked out of the corner of his eye to see if any of the other men really noticed. He hoped that he would stop shaking and feeling nauseated if he would just keep riding and let matters rest. His hand really started stinging as sweat ran into the cut, so he removed his kerchief and tied it around his palm.

They rode closer to the hiding place of the Colt children, each man with a burning desire to eliminate them. What would happen if anyone learned a seven-year-old boy had outwitted a gang of killers and wounded two of them? They'd be laughed at from Texas to Montana.

After an hour the would-be kidnappers made it to the big bowl, and each man looked around in awe. Nobody could ride into a steep-sided, sheer rock valley and not feel impressed, even intimidated, by the surroundings. The bowl was a mile across, and patches of glacial ice dotted the rocky landscape. The rocks beneath these white patches were dark from the constantly melting glaciers which fed the scattered small lakes all over the bottom of the bowl. There were no trees at this altitude and the wind usually howled, but at the moment it was clear and sunny. The peaks went almost straight up over a thousand feet on three sides and blotted out most of the sky.

Johnny rode among the boulders, scouring the area for any sign on the rocks. Finally he found what he was looking for. He signaled the others to come ahead. Aramus pulled his Henry carbine from its boot, cocked it, and held the rifle ready across the swell of his saddle.

Chris chuckled and stood, a little tear ran down his cheek, and he quickly wiped it away with the back of his hand. He walked over to Charley, who had a small smokeless fire with a pot of coffee burning. She offered Chris some bacon and biscuits.

He said, "We won't often get lunch on this journey, so we better enjoy it every time we can."

She said, "Did you work out all the signs?"

Colt said, "Yes, ma'am. Can't tell you how proud I am of that boy of mine. He apparently set a couple traps for these fellas. That one that Tex told you was so tall, he got scared out of the saddle down there by those bushes. He dived right into the bushes and got stuck on two of the pointed sticks Joseph had stuck in the ground and had pointed towards the trail. He bled a lot and moved around in a lot of pain.

Then over there, as much as I hate to see animals hurt, a horse got run over by some runaway boulders. Joseph had rolled big rocks into a pile up there and had them held back by a log on an angle with a rope tied to it. When he pulled the rope, the rocks went down and broke a horse's leg, and they had to shoot it."

"Shame about the horse. Though it's good one of them no longer has a mount," she said. "How about that son of yours? I told you before, Christopher, the apples don't fall very far from the tree. Which way do we head?"

Colt said, "Up. The only problem is that the Indian with them was a scout. I can tell by the way he moves and checks sign. He will know— in fact, any of them with trail knowledge would know—that they went up into the rocks to hide their trail. Let's get after them and be ready. We're close."

"Do you think they might have gotten them?"

Colt said, "Not if that boy of mine keeps coming up with tricks like he did here."

The men sat around their horses and looked at all the tracks where the girls and horses had been holed up.

Pointing, Johnny said, "Look."

Under a rock was a blue-and-white plaid

gingham sun bonnet. It had the edges held down by rocks, and the top was tied together like a bag. It was placed well down under a rock, so it was hard to get a hold of. Phineas jumped down and reached for the bag. He undid the string holding it together. He heard the rattle a split second before he screamed with pain and withdrew his hand out of the bonnet, a large rattler attached to the meaty part of his palm. The fangs had gone in deep, and Phineas was once again in severe pain.

"Sumbitch!' he howled. "Them little . . .! Them little . . .!"

Aramus calmly said, "Better hesh an git you a tourneeket on thet, right quick, or you gonna die."

These words seemed to hit Phineas in the pit of his stomach, and he sat down meekly. Aramus dismounted and splinted the hand, cutting an X on each fang mark with his bowie knife. He sucked golden venom, mixed with blood from the wounds, and spat it on the ground.

Johnny walked up with a large chunk of ice and tied it over the wound with two kerchiefs. "We learn ice, if you have, helps make better, but you get sick, Phineas."

Phineas's color drained from his face. "How sick?"

Aramus said, "Yo be crappin' yo pants plenty and yo stomach is gwine ta hurt bad, and yo is gonna git a fever and sweats an . . ."

Phineas interrupted, "Forget it! I don't want to know. Get me on my horse and let's get out of here."

Buck poured some whiskey on the bites with his good arm, and the gang mounted up.

Johnny turned and looked at Aramus, saying, "Snake-that-sings not live this high. Boy carried snake up here to make trap. Boy is smart, like man who knows mountains. Sometimes, boy hides trail good, too."

Aramus said, "Wal, we's gwine ta kill the little brat and dem little girls, too."

Phineas snarled, "I wanna kill the boy. He's mine."

Aramus laughed, "Ef'n ya wants to, but it looks like he done kilt you awready mebbe."

Phineas gave the black man a queer look, and the color drained from his face again. He felt weak and sick to his stomach, but he wasn't sure it was from the snake bite. He clucked to his horse and kicked it in the ribs. The ground waved in front of him as wild onions, biscuits, and beef jerky started rising up his esophagus. His knees started shaking, and he wondered how many miles he could go.

*   *   *

Joseph led the three girls out, not trying to cover his trail right now. When he saw an opportunity, he would try to come up with something to slow the pursuers down. He kept thinking, What would Pa do?

The little boy was very scared, but he knew that he had the greatest father and mother in the world, and even if his ma wasn't here anymore, she was watching him from Heaven and would always do so. He was a Colt, and he was going to act like a Colt.

CHAPTER 5

Getting Home

Joseph was trying to figure out what to do next when they rode by a "glory hole." Although the Sangre de Cristo Mountain range was extremely desolate and the upper reaches near and above timberline were especially unforgiving, it was still surprising how much of the terrain had been covered by prospectors. They'd dug glory holes all over the mountains, wherever they suspected for one reason or another they would find riches in silver or gold. These glory holes were generally large hand-dug holes in the ground or rock, maybe ten to thirty paces across and from five to twenty feet deep. Not finding what was desired, the prospector would desert the glory hole, dug with pick, shovel, and double-tree, and go on to another location.

The hole that Joseph found was in the tree line and one ridgeline over from the outlaws.

He wondered if he would have time to set a booby trap. Joseph decided to try it, telling the girls to stay mounted and flee if the outlaws appeared at the top of the ridge. Ignoring him, the three girls jumped down as soon as they realized what he was doing. They all quickly searched for long, thin branches to put across the hole. There were always plenty of blow-downs near the timberline because of the numerous avalanches and storms at that high elevation. The kids soon had plenty of long branches, and they laid them across the hole one way and then crossed an equal number of branches in sideways. They then started tearing up clumps of moist soil covered with thick, high grasses and set them on the fragile framework.

They carefully tried to cover the edges of the hole and arrange the grassy clumps to look as natural as possible. Satisfied that they had camouflaged their trap, they retreated into the woods. Joseph led the girls up the ridge inside the woods, and at the top they stopped and looked back into the valley. They had a clear view of the trap, although it was a good distance away. They tied the horses just over the ridge and out of sight. One thing Joseph noticed that bothered him was the rocky tailing so visible just downhill from the trap. Every glory hole had tailings comprised of a dirt or rock pile, usually at its downhill side from all the earth that had been dug out of the ground.

Brenna said, "Shh, look."

Joseph grinned as the outlaws topped the crest. He was proud of his little sister and cousins for their help. He saw that he never would have finished the trap in time if he had prepared it by himself. All four watched with interest.

Rebecca said, "Joseph, what do we do if somebody doesn't fall in the hole?"

Joseph said, "I wanted to go up higher and try to make a big fire that Pa could see, but they are too close. No matter what, we are going to try to make it down the mountain as fast as we can and run the horses to the ranch. Uncle Joshua will make sure we're safe."

Emily said, "I wish Uncle Chris was here now."

Brenna said, "Well, he's not, so we have to be brave and act like Colts, okay?"

Emily said, "Okay, but I'm hungry."

"That's okay," Joseph said, smiling. "We'll eat at the ranch."

While they watched the outlaws getting closer to the trap, Joseph set up a rock signal that they were headed straight downhill toward the ranch, and he stuck two tacks in a branch on a sapling nearby. He knew his pa must have found one of the shiny tacks anyway by now. Joseph had put them high on trees every chance he got.

The children got more excited as they saw Johnny, out in front of the rest, approach the hole. Joseph sighed audibly as the scout left the trail and rode around the spot where the trap was. It didn't look like he had spotted it, but was just leaving the trail, watching closely for tracks. The rest approached the hole with Aramus in the lead.

Joseph said, "He's the one that killed Ma. I hope he falls in and cracks his noggin open on a rock, and all his brains and blood spills out, and worms eat his body in the hole."

Aramus was just three steps away, checking from side to side with no clue about the trap. Johnny Shouts-at-the-Sky looked just in time and yelled at Aramus, "Stop! Don't move!"

Aramus yelled, "Whoa!" He jerked back on his reins sharply.

The steel dust gelding looked to be smiling when the curb bit pulled back on both sides of his mouth. The horse opened and closed his mouth several times, trying to relieve the pressure, but he stopped dead and backed up two steps.

The children were disappointed, and Joseph led them over the hill to the horses. Mounting up, he said, "Come on. We have to get down the mountain quick. They're really gonna be mad now."

At the trap, Johnny slid up next to Aramus and dismounted.

As Johnny started to pick up a large rock, Aramus said, "What de hell is yo probbem?"

Johnny didn't reply. Grunting, he hefted a melon-sized rock and tossed it forward onto the trap. Several sticks broke with loud cracks as the rock and several clumps of clod and weed crashed through the middle of the trap, leaving a wine-barrel-sized hole in the center. All the outlaws gave each other looks of astonishment.

Watching carefully for more booby traps, the gang of outlaws followed the tracks up to the kids' perch overlooking the pit on the far ridge. They found the tracks where the two horses had headed down the mountain at a good clip.

"Damn, Sam!" Aramus said, "We's gits ta git down dis mountain quick or they's gwine ta makes it back ta dat ranch. We doesn't want ta go back dere."

Too-Tall, who had been in too much pain to say much, had to speak out. "Aramus, do you want it on yer headstone thet a little boy out-foxed ya?"

Normally Aramus would have put his gang member in his place for questioning his decision, but he thought about the snake, the rock slide, the pit, and said, "Good point. We take our time. We'll catch the li'l rug rats."

If only Joseph had known this, he would have slowed down greatly. The kids were hurrying down the mountain as fast as they could. Emily rode behind Rebecca and Brenna behind her big brother. They really sped up when there was a break in the tall trees at one point and they could see all the buildings of the Coyote Run. The ranch was about three thousand feet lower than them and six miles away, but from the mountain it looked much closer.

The kids broke out of the trees and headed down a ridge covered with scrub oaks. The leafy branches brushed against their legs and arms as they sped downhill, at a steeper angle now. It was one of these branches that was their undoing. Joseph knew where he was going. He was looking for a long-used Ute Indian hunting trail, which was also used a lot by prospectors. It would take them past Brush Creek Lakes and down to their own property. He had followed the trail several times, accompanying his father and Man Killer up into the big range. Unfortunately, as the kids scraped through one of the denser thickets of scrub oak, one of the branches snapped past Joseph's right foot and snagged Brenna's. Her leg was pulled back sharply, and she flew off the horse with a scream. She hit the ground and rolled rapidly downhill, through some undergrowth, and over a lip right onto the middle of the trail. She landed on her back, the wind knocked out of her, and her head hit the ground. Then everything went black.

The children jumped off their horses, and Emily started screaming in panic when she saw Brenna lying motionless on the ground. Joseph ran up to her and grabbed her upper arms, shaking her violently.

He said firmly, "Be quiet!"

Emily sobbed and said, "I'm sorry."

Joseph said, "It's okay. Brenna will be fine."

He believed that, too. Joseph had been raised that way, to believe that everything would always turn out right. When it didn't turn out right, he was taught to turn it into something right.

The children looked all around desperately, each one apparently looking for an answer to their dilemma. Joseph spoke softly to his little sister, but she did not respond.

He said, "Jump on Spot and run down the hill. There's a creek down there. Wet some cloths quick and bring them back."

Rebecca ran to her horse and made a running mount on it. She was back up the ridge within ten minutes. Brenna was still unconscious but started stirring when the cold water from Joseph's kerchief was placed on her face. She suddenly sat bolt upright, eyes open, and looked all around in amazement.

"What happened, Joseph?"

He said, "You fell off Spot and got a bump on the head. How do you feel?"

Brenna smiled, saying, "Fine." Yet there was a faraway look in her eyes, and it concerned her brother.

Up above, Too-Tall's long left leg caught on a scrub oak branch, and he moaned in pain. "Son of a buck!"

Hearing this, the children gave each other startled looks. Joseph and Rebecca grabbed Brenna under the arms and took her to Rebecca's horse.

Joseph said, "Becky, mount up behind her and hold her, even if she talks fine. Emily, you ride behind Becky and hold on tight."

They climbed up in their saddle, and Joseph mounted up on Spot.

Becky, said, "What are you doing?"

Joseph said, "I'm going to lead them away, back up the mountain."

Rebecca started to speak, but Joseph cut her off. "Don't argue! No time! Take this trail downhill. It will take you right to a gate in our fence. You'll see the ranch houses way off. When you get in the pasture, run your horse, but walk until then. I'll keep them after me. Go!"

Joseph turned his horse and ran right back up through the scrub oaks toward the outlaws. Rebecca heard two men yelling up the ridge as the boy was spotted, followed by a gunshot. She stayed to the trail and headed downhill toward the ranch. As soon as she rounded the bend, she could see it again far off, and that gave her renewed hope. Yet she looked back, tears flooding her cheeks and eyes as she worried about her cousin. He was running right into the lion's jaws.

Joseph spotted the men and took to running at an angle uphill but back toward the trail. When he hit it, he knew he would go faster than the outlaws because they would have to angle through the scrub oak. Johnny, in the lead, took a snap shot at him. In response, Joseph swung one leg over the horse's back and while his right hand held the saddle horn, he held under the horse's neck with his left hand, an old Indian trick taught him by Man Killer. Spot seemed to sense the desperation in their flight and carried his young charge as fast as he could.

When Chris and Charley heard the first gunshot, they looked at each other, eyes open in alarm, and both charged headlong toward the sound of the gunshots.

All the gang members spurred their horses as fast as they could through the giant scrub oak thicket. Not far to the south they could see smoke curling up out of chimneys of houses in Westcliffe, Silver Cliff, and Rosita.

Joseph laid out along the horse's neck and kept urging Spot, "Faster!" All the outlaws seemed to start shooting at him at once. Bullets whizzed all about him, making cracking sounds.

Joseph didn't know where the trial led, but he suspected that it went up and over a pass between peaks into the San Luis Valley. If he made it over, he would head down and across the valley for Saguache. He had met a lawman there before when he came by his ranch to talk with Joseph's pa. The boy thought about how much he wished his pa was there now.

The chase continued, with the determined

criminals not giving up. Spot was lathered up and breathing heavily, so Joseph reined him back to a trot, then a fast walk. He had to let the horse get his air at this high altitude or the horse would cramp up and die.

Joseph came into an area of thick trees and numerous little glacial creeks, running down on either side. A large cracking sound went by his left ear, and he ducked low over Spot's neck. The horse took off even before Joseph kicked him. They galloped along the trail and broke out into bright daylight, right at the edge of the timberline. Before them stretched alpine meadows, dotted with little yellow and purple flowers. As Joseph rounded a bend, he looked back at the pursuers running headlong on lathered horses. Almost too late, he turned back around in time to see the washout in the trail.

To his right was a sheer rock wall about six feet high, and to his left was a drop-off of a hundred feet straight down. The trail had been washed out by some storm. The horse saw the cut out at the same time as Joseph and slid to a stop right at the washout. Joseph had nowhere to go. He jumped out of the saddle and pulled forth his knife, facing his attackers.

A shout came up from the outlaws as they saw they had their prey cornered. They slowed to a walk. Joseph felt a lump forming in his throat as the men pulled their rifles from their saddle boots.

Two of the men raised their guns and Aramus raised his hand, pulling out a long knife and smiling menacingly.

"Ah put yo ma under wif dis knife, boy," he yelled, "now it's yo turn."

Joseph sneered at all the men defiantly, thrusting his jaw out, and said, "I ain't scared. I'll die like a man. My name is Joseph Colt, and my pa will hunt down each and every one of you and kill you all. The worms will eat your guts, too."

Johnny, for the first time in his life, felt a little remorse, for he certainly was amazed at this little boy's courage. Being the one tracking Joseph, he already had tremendous respect for the lad's ingenuity.

Aramus just laughed and said, "Too bad, li'l boy, but yer pa ain't here to save yer scrawny hide right now!"

Just then a shot rang out from above and then another. The gang looked uphill, and someone yelled, "It's Colt!"

Forgetting the boy, the gang spun their horses around and took off back down the trail. Chris and Charley Colt came charging down the ridge, firing carbines on the run. Tears of joy ran down

Joseph's face and his knees buckled under him in excitement.

Chris and Charley made the trail finally and cantered up to Joseph. Jumping off his horse, Colt ran to his son and picked the boy up in his arms, holding him tightly. They could see the gang of outlaws circling the canyon across from them, over a half mile away now. Joseph sobbed on Chris's shoulder and held him tightly.

Colt said, "I'm so proud of you, son. Where are the girls?"

Joseph said, "We were going down the mountain, and Brenna fell off Spot and got knocked out. She's awake now, but acting goofy. You know, like Tex acted after that old roan stallion kicked him in the raspberries that time."

Joseph got a shocked look on his face and looked at his aunt as his face turned beet red.

He said, "I'm sorry, Aunt Charlotte. I didn't mean to say that it front of you."

She dismounted and said, "I'll forgive you if I can have a giant hug."

He ran into her arms and laid his head on her shoulder while she stroked his hair. Tears trickled down Charley's cheeks.

"You are quite a young man, Joseph Colt," she said.

119

Chris said, "Son, we have to know about the girls."

Joseph replied, "They're safe, Pa. I sent them down this trail to the ranch. I told Rebecca not to let go of Brenna no matter what and not to run the horse until they go through the gate on our pasture."

Charlotte said, "Why are you up here?"

"Because he wanted the killers to chase him, so the girls could make it back to the ranch safely," Chris explained.

Charley held Joseph at arm's length and smiled at him in wonder. She gave him several giant kisses and squeezed him tightly again.

Tears flowing freely down her face now, she whispered, "God bless you, Joseph Colt. God bless you."

Chris winked at Joseph, who gave his father an embarrassed look over his aunt's shoulder.

After they had mounted up, Colt looked the young Colt in the eye and said, "No father has ever had a finer son."

He took off at a slow trot back down the trail, explaining over his shoulder, "Come on. We have to find the girls."

It took a half hour to catch up with the girls. They were just reaching the gate on the Colt property. Chris checked Brenna and told Charley that she needed to get her to the doctor immediately.

Charley said, "Where are you going, Chris? We're at the ranch."

Joseph said, "I told those men that my pa would hunt them all down and kill them."

Chris mounted up and said, "That just about covers it, sis."

Charley said. "When will we hear from you, Chris?"

Colt said, "When my work's done. You'll see me again. Take care of my kids, Charley?"

"Of course." She smiled. "Give 'em hell, Christopher Colt, from both barrels."

Colt turned War Bonnet and headed back up the trail.

CHAPTER 6

One by One

Chris Colt did not pick up their new trail again for two days. Once they crossed over the big range, they headed south and crossed back over to the Wet Mountain Valley side over Medano Pass. Maybe they figured it would throw him off, but Chris Colt was a man on a mission and nothing would stop him.

Back at the Coyote Run, over the protests of his beautiful wife, Jennifer Banta, and Charlotte Colt, Man Killer mounted up on his big black Appaloosa with the white blanket on his rump.

Joshua and Tex would not speak as the young warrior rode off to help is blood brother Chris Colt. He was still experiencing headaches, but Joshua and Tex knew they would be wasting their breath trying to talk him out of going. Everyone watched as the young man rode toward Spread Eagle, now a mile away. He was about to cross the last creek before going into the big timber. The horse jumped over the creek and Jennifer screamed as they saw Man Killer fly through the air and disappear in the tall meadow grass.

"Quick, mount up," Charley said.

But Joshua calmly said, "Just wait a minute, Charlotte."

They kept watching as the horse turned and jumped back across the creek and apparently walked up to where his master lay on the ground. After several minutes, they saw Man Killer grab the stirrups and pull himself up into a sitting position, then a standing position. It took another ten full minutes, but he somehow managed to crawl up the saddle using his arms and he headed back toward them. Man Killer's body slumped in defeat as he rode back, but every person watching admired him greatly.

When he reached the assembled watchers he started to dismount, obviously trying to hide a great deal of pain. He struggled to get off the horse and Jennifer started forward but Joshua grabbed her arm and gently held her back. She stopped and watched with the others. Man Killer slowly and painfully made it off the horse. He smiled at his wife.

Man Killer said, "The eagle wants to fly into the storm, but his wings are broken."

His eyes rolled up in his head, and he fainted, as Joshua ran forward and caught him before he hit the ground.

Colt followed the gang as they wound their way along the face of several mountains, then headed up again by Marble Mountain. They were headed toward Crestone Needle's, the most dangerous terrain in the Sangre de Cristos. The going got rougher and rougher, and shortly before day's end, Chris Colt found himself following their trail across a deep avalanche chute. He was concerned as he looked almost directly overhead a thousand feet up and saw a giant snow cornice hanging above.

Chris was halfway across when the gang members peered out from their hiding place behind some rocks. Everyone had a rifle in their hands, and they all aimed at the unstable glacier.

Aramus chuckled and said, "The Colt are bout ta learn bout traps. Ready, fire!"

A volley of shots rang out, answered almost immediately by a low rumbling sound. The outlaws sprinted for their horses, still intimidated by the legendary gunfighter.

Chris Colt knew instantly that he was in deep trouble. He couldn't make it across or go back, so he wheeled War Bonnet and rode straight downhill. Above him the giant snowslide started gaining momentum, dislodging boulders in its path. Hundreds of thousands of tons of snow cascaded downward. As the big horse went straight down the slope, Chris Colt leaned backward, his back only an inch over the horse's rump. Colt pulled his bandanna up over his mouth and nose, because he knew most people died in an avalanche from having their mouths and nostrils filled firmly with fine powder snow, actually choking them to death. Without being told, War Bonnet ran out on a ten-foot rock outcropping and dived off. Thirty feet he fell into deep snow, his master still on his back. Just before the giant wall of snow hit, now traveling at almost two hundred miles per hour, Colt wheeled the horse under a large rock outcropping and dismounted, holding the paint's reins. He placed his hat over the horse's nostrils and held it there as the mountain of snow and rocks shot past, over, and around them. The rumbling was like a thousand freight trains, but it ended before long. Even on the steep-sided mountain Colt found himself and his horse neck-deep in snow. Removing his hat from War Bonnet's nose, he stopped and looked skyward and offered up a prayer of thanks.

"Honey, I know you're watching, and I just want you to know that I'll always love you. There will never be another."

As if in response, a bald eagle suddenly flew off of one of the peaks above and swirled in lazy circles overhead. Chris Colt smiled broadly, a tear in one eye. "Thanks for answering. I'll get them all. I swear it."

The eagle flew out of sight and Colt wondered if that was a sign he was wrong. He thought about it and decided he didn't care; they were all going to die.

He surveyed the situation. He and his horse were stuck high up on a mountain. They were neck-deep in snow perched on the side of a nearly sheer cliff. And night was coming on.

Using the stock of his rifle, Colt started shoveling out a snow cave for him and his horse to spend the night in. As he did, he noticed a piece of wood sticking up out of the snow some twenty paces away. He left War Bonnet and swam along the snow's surface to the wood. Once there, he dug around it. Some miner had made a windlass to lower himself into his glory hole.

Here it was, high above the timberline, a

source of wood to get Colt and War Bonnet through the night. Colt tore the rotten contraption into pieces and started throwing them over near his horse. It took a good hour, but he soon had a fine supply of firewood and a snow cave to stay in. War Bonnet would go without food, but Colt had plenty for himself, even coffee, and they would be reasonably warm.

That night Chris Colt dreamed about his wife and children. In the morning, he awakened to find a bright sun shining on the snow. Water was pouring off rocks everywhere. Colt knew that he couldn't worry about the outlaws. He had to concentrate solely on survival in a situation like this. He waited until midafternoon to make his bid to escape the snow pile, but the going was too tough, especially on War Bonnet. Colt knew that it would take several more days of hot sun for the snow to melt enough to release them.

Yet then the trail would be hopelessly cold.

Chris finally came up with an idea. Using his rifle butt as a shovel again, he started digging a path up to the top of the rock outcropping. Darkness was approaching when he finally got the horse up on top of the outcropping. He mounted up and slowly walked the horse forward to the edge of the drop-off. Thirty feet below them was his snow cave, but beyond that the mountainside got even steeper. Far down below, big trees were broken off and uprooted from the force of the avalanche.

Colt backed the big horse up in the narrow snow trail he had made and patted him on the neck. Colt tied his hat on, using his kerchief, and made sure his saddlebags were tied shut and the thongs were over his pistol hammers.

He said, "Well, boy, this might kill us, but if we stay, we'll die, and it just might save us. Ready to try?"

The horse reached out with one hoof and pawed at the rock. Colt tightened on the reins a second, and anticipating the new adventure, the horse reared a little and took off. At the edge of the rock outcropping he leapt with his powerful rump, muscles propelling them well out past the snow cave. The two fell and fell and hit the powdery mountainside tumbling and sliding downward. At some point Colt became disengaged from the horse, but the two kept falling and sliding down the mountainside. The mountain was much steeper here. Colt fought to keep alert, so he could dive this way and that to avoid rocks sticking up out of the snow. The big horse fought to stay upright. The trees down below got larger and larger, and the two finally came to rest. Colt made his way over to the horse and checked War Bonnet's legs. One was cut and bleeding a little, but the horse seemed sound. The snow here was five feet deep, and the ground had leveled off almost.

Chris climbed up in the saddle and urged the horse toward a nearby windswept ridge. War Bonnet lunged forward in a bucking motion through the snow. They made it onto the ridge, where the snow was less than a foot deep. Once there, Colt had his horse trot down the ridgeline, not stopping until he had descended over two thousand feet and they were in warm sunshine. Chris rode until he found a large meadow with good grass. He unsaddled his horse, rubbing him down with dry grass, and let the big paint graze and relax. Colt would let the horse renew himself and then continue on his quest. He had lost so much time already that waiting until the next morning would not make that much difference.

It was another two days before Chris Colt sorted out and followed the trail of the outlaws. He didn't like what he found. At one point, presumably while their wounded rested, they had sent two men back to look at the avalanche site through a telescope. They must have seen Colt riding War Bonnet down the ridgeline, because someone had decided that they should all split up and ride out in different directions. Chris Colt was upset by this, but it did not matter. He'd just have to hunt them down one by one.

The hardest to find would be the scout, so Colt decided to go after him first. The scout's tracks from their camp at Hermit Lake led off to the south to Music Pass, then west toward the Great Sand Dunes. Chris Colt knew that the scout was smart enough to not even attempt to make it look like he was going to go east and cross the Wet Mountain Valley, since he had to go miles to the south to cross over the big range.

Chris Colt tried to figure out which way Johnny Shouts-at-the-Sky would go. That was one of the biggest challenges of scouting, guessing a trail by figuring out your prey's motives or intents. He knew that Johnny would not try to lose him by going across the Great Sand Dunes, since finding his trail would be fairly easy. Tracking him across the floor of the San Luis Valley would also not be hard, since it was a large, flat valley. If he was heading toward the Great Sand Dunes, he would be hard-pressed to lose Colt anywhere close, so he must be crossing the valley, Chris figured. If that was the case, he would be going toward Wolf Creek Pass and headed toward the four corners area, where Utah, Colorado, Arizona, and New Mexico all met. Once he got to, and especially over, Wolf Creek Pass, it would be much easier to lose Chris Colt because it was heavily wooded.

Colt took off hell-bent for leather southwest. He would board the next train, west, bypassing Wolf Creek and ending up in Durango. From there he would start backtracking. He knew that word would be out that he was hunting his wife's killers, and the scout knew that he would stand out more than the others.

At Durango, Colt boarded War Bonnet at the livery stable in town and headed for the busiest saloon he could find. He went in, looked for a corner table, sat down facing the door, and ordered an iced beer from a friendly-acting barkeep. A fancy lady spotted Colt and sauntered up to his table. She smiled and set her foot up on the chair next to him and lifted the edge of her bright red dress to remove a small cigar from her stocking. She looked at Colt coyly as she stuck the cigar between her lips.

"Got a light, mister?"

Obliging her, Colt lit the cigar and blew out the match.

She sat down smiling, but Colt said, "I don't want company, ma'am."

She pouted and started to argue when the barkeep brought Colt's beer over. "He just lost his wife, Cookie, leave him be."

Embarrassed, she walked off. Colt nodded at the bartender and winked.

This man had known who he was when he walked in the door. Colt got this kind of reaction all the time, but it always surprised him. He drank his beer slowly, waiting for the crowd to thin out. After a half hour things got slow, so he called the bartender over. The man brought a fresh beer, and Colt motioned for the man to sit down. He was a short, balding man with a big walrus mustache, ruddy cheeks, and a twinkle in his eyes.

Colt said, "Thanks for your help. I didn't want to have to be impolite with her. Maybe you can help me with something else. I'm looking for an Indian, probably wearing something an ex-scout would wear, maybe cavalry pants. He wouldn't look like the ones around here."

The bartender said, "Not a Ute, huh?"

Colt said, "No, I'm guessing maybe Crow or Arikara. He does wear cavalry boots and cavalry spurs. Rides a big horse, black mane and tail, but I don't know what color the body is."

The bartender said, "Johnny Shouts-at-the-Sky, rides a big mouse-colored gelding, black mane and tail. He's Arikara. Used to scout down at Fort Union. His brother married a Ute and lives out east toward Pagosa Springs. Actually, a little south halfway between here and there."

Colt said, "Ignacio?"

The bartender said, "Yes, sir, near there. You know Ignacio?"

Colt said, "Yep." He got up and tossed a couple coins to the bartender saying, "Thanks, partner. Keep the change."

Colt got out of there and headed for the livery stable. He would ride hard and make camp at Chimney Rock, halfway between Durango and Pagosa Springs, then head south for the Southern Ute reservation in the morning.

It was midafternoon when Chris Colt rode into the Ute village. He had many friends among the tribe, and he soon learned where Johnny Shouts-at-the-Sky was staying. When Chris Colt rode into the village, he was greeted by the sight of Johnny sitting atop his gray, but without a saddle on it.

Johnny had heard Colt was coming and knew that there would be no place to hide. He had already done a sweat lodge and that morning had sung his death song. He now had stripped

133

off all white man's clothing and wore a breechcloth, moccasins, bone hair pipe breast-plate, and beaded bands around each large bi-ceps. He also carried a thick buffalo bullhide shield, a lance, and wore a knife at his waist.

Colt stopped, and Johnny yelled at him, "Colt, will you fight me the Indian way? With guns, I have no chance."

Colt said, "Did my wife have a chance?"

Johnny said, "Yes, she could have given in, but she wanted the young ones to flee."

Colt said, "But did my wife have a chance?"

Johnny said, "No, she did not!"

Chris lit a cigarillo and puffed on it thought-fully. He finally said, "Yes, I will fight you in the way of your people."

"It will be an honor to kill you and take away your medicine!" Johnny shouted. "The mighty Colt is a great warrior."

Colt merely said, "Yeah, well give me a minute!"

The entire village was gathering now, making a circle around the two. Colt rode his horse to a young boy with a smile on his face. Colt handed him the reins. "Hold him for me. If I am killed he is your horse."

The boy's eyes opened wide in wonder, but

he said, "I do not want your horse. I want Colt
to live. You are the Great One."

Touched, Chris reached in his saddlebag and
brought out a bag of coffee and a bag of tobacco.
He carried them over to the chief and handed
them to him. He said, "I did not want to come
to your village and cause trouble, but he is one
of the men who killed my wife."

The chief accepted the gifts and replied, "I
know this, and this is a good thing that you do.
My people do not make war on women."

Colt said, "I know this. You are mighty
warriors."

He stripped off his guns and shirt, then
slipped off his boots and spurs and replaced
them with soft-soled moccasins from his
saddlebags.

He had no lance, so he looked around, and
one of the Utes came up to him and offered his.
Colt smiled and nodded. Saying thanks was not
the Indian way.

As he faced Johnny, the Arikara jerked up on
his reins, indicating he wanted to be mounted.
Chris shrugged and walked over to War Bonnet.
He reached inside his saddlebags again, dug
around, and pulled out a tin can full of peaches
and some hard candy. These he handed to the
boy. The lad's face lit up like a Christmas tree.

Colt grabbed the saddlehorn and swung up into the saddle. Sensing the upcoming battle, War Bonnet started prancing and gave a little rear. Colt took the offered lance from the Ute warrior and spun the paint around twice.

He whispered to the big horse, "Here we go, boy. You trust me, and we'll do fine."

Johnny reared on his horse and gave out a loud war whoop and charged at Colt. The lawman gave out a bloodcurdling scream himself and he charged toward the oncoming Arikara renegade. As they came closer, Johnny raised his lance overhead as if he was about to throw it at Colt as they passed. They were closing in, less than fifteen feet apart, and still Colt was yelling, so forcefully Johnny looked unnerved.

As Johnny's arm started to come forward with the lance, Colt drove his left knee into War Bonnet's shoulder and squeezed hard with his right calf on the horse's rib cage. The horse, as always, responded immediately to the leg aids, and suddenly lurched to the left. The lance passed harmlessly past the man and horse, and War Bonnet slammed chest first into the mouse-colored horse, knocking his head and neck sideways and driving him up and over backward. Johnny rolled out of the way a split second before the hooves of the big horse crashed down on him.

In the meantime, Chris Colt reined the horse so he was facing his grounded enemy. Blood was pouring from Johnny's nostrils, and Colt nodded. He kicked the horse in the flanks and he charged ahead, yelling again. He dived headlong at the Indian outlaw, crashing into the man's chest, much as his horse had done to the red man's horse. Johnny was knocked backward and got up slowly, shaking his head.

Colt had also knocked himself silly, and his knees felt a little rubbery, but he knew that would pass.

Johnny pulled his big knife out and waved it menacingly. Chris Colt pulled out his big bowie knife in response. He stood, his feet shoulder-width apart and held the knife blade up in his right hand. Chris would fight by countering, figuring that the other man would be aggressive and might attack too quickly. Johnny circled to Colt's left but would not come within striking range. The Arikara stopped and started circling in the other direction. He was wetting his lips and tossing the knife back and forth from hand to hand. Chris Colt knew by these signs alone that the brave was very scared.

Colt stood straight up, unmoving. "Tell me

the names of the others in the gang and where I can find them, and I will kill you quickly."

With false bravado Johnny laughed and said, "I do not tell nothing, Colt. I will not die. You will die."

Chris said, "You had your chance."

He lunged at Johnny, but the Arikara danced away. Johnny retreated every time Chris went after him. Then Johnny started circling again.

Colt again stopped and said, "This is your last chance: Tell me the names of all the members of your gang and where I can find them, and I will let you live. If you don't tell me now, I will kill you and go find them myself."

Johnny laughed nervously and entertained the thought of telling Colt, but he felt it would make him lose face in front of his brother and the Utes. "I will steal your spirit from your body and catch it, Colt."

"You had your chance. See if you can catch this."

Chris Colt flipped his knife up and caught it by the blade. His arm went forward in a whipping motion, and the knife spun around twice in the air, burying itself to the hilt in the left side of Johnny's chest. The scout's eyes opened wide, and he looked down at the handle of the knife sticking out of his chest. He saw tiny bubbles of red liquid seeping out around the blade. He looked up at Colt in shock. Grabbing the handle, he pulled as hard as he could. The blade would not come out of his chest. He stood on his tiptoes and walked around in a small circle, still pulling. Then he dropped his hands, palms outward, shrugged his shoulders, and walked away from Colt and the others, a vacant stare in his eyes. In his mind, as he walked those last ten steps, Johnny saw Shirley Colt, a giant knife in her hand, and she plunged a knife into his chest over and over. In this living daydream, he kept trying to scream, "No!" but nothing would come out of his mouth. His tenth step away from Colt was the last he ever made. He saw the ground rushing at his open eyes, and they did not blink when his face crashed into it.

Johnny heard his brother speak in Arikara, saying. "Oh, no, my brother is dead."

Colt looked at him, saying, "He helped kill my wife. Blood for blood. My fight is not with you, unless you want it to be. What's your answer?"

Johnny's brother shook his head. "It was your right."

Colt walked to the chief, and they grasped each other's forearms, shaking in Indian fashion.

He said, "A man that makes war on women does not know how to fight against a man."

The chief grinned and nodded. "If I want to shoot the rabbit that runs, I whistle like the hawk. Thinking it is to die, the rabbit stops and opens his eyes very wide. If I hunt the great bear, I do not whistle."

The young boy led War Bonnet to Colt and handed him the reins.

Chris smiled and pulled out a gold double eagle and pressed it into the boy's palm. As the boy ran to show off his coin to his parents, Chris Colt mounted up and rode out of the village.

Chris Colt got far away from the village and made a camp on the Florida River to rest from his brief but exhausting combat ordeal. Chris Colt was a legend to everyone, but in actuality, he was simply a man. After resting up for a day, out of sight of anyone, Colt decided to return to Durango and see if he could learn anything about any of the other gang members. He would, if he got a lead, board another train there.

The first place Colt visited was the same saloon where he had got the information on Johnny Shouts-at-the-Sky. The same bartender came over, a smile on his face, and set an ice cold beer down. Colt smiled at him and nodded, tossing him a coin. Again, Colt sat at a corner table, back to the wall. The bartender waited on two more customers at the bar and returned to Colt's table.

He said, "Did you find Johnny, Marshal Colt?"

Chris smiled and said, "Thanks for the beer. It's cold."

The barkeep got the hint, cleared his throat, and returned to the bar. No sooner had he done that than a man, dressed in buckskins and furs came in and bellied up to the bar. He was not only a mountain man, but also a mountain of a man.

"Whiskey!" he roared, "Hey, barkeep! Hear the latest about Chris Colt?"

The bartender looked over at Colt, who dipped his head so his hat brim hid his face.

The mountain man went on, "Old Chris Colt is huntin' down them what done in his wife. He rides into a Ute village just two days ago down to Ignacio. Fights Johnny Shouts-at-the-Sky with lance and bowie and kills him like he was a weasel in a henhouse. Accordin' to the Utes, Colt didn't even break a sweat. He even give Johnny a chance to spill his guts about the other men."

The man threw back a shot, poured another, shivered, and tilted his head back with another shot of amber liquid.

"Burr, that's good sippin' whiskey," the mountain man exclaimed. "I'll tell you what, old Chris Colt will hunt 'em all down, and kill every man-jack of 'em, and they deserve it, too. You hear what his woman done? Talk about brass raspberries."

The bartender looked over at Colt nervously and interjected, "Yes, sir, we all heard and don't want to talk about it, okay. How's the trapping up in the San Juan's? That where you been?"

The man said, "South a Wolf Creek. Ah, the beaver ain't what they used to be and the buffaler, too. You know what I'm doin' now? Huntin' grizz. Them dudes back East will pay a mint for grizzly claws.

"I can make more doin' that and make ranchers happy than trappin' tons a beaver. I been shootin' me some painters, too, and trapped me a few bobcat."

The bartender felt relieved. He now had the big man talking about trapping.

Unfortunately, the mountain man had another shot and went right back to Shirley Colt, "That woman a Chris Colt's. She done held on to Aramus Randall while he sticks her over and over with a knife so her kids could git away. Wouldn't let go, then takes a bite outta his cheek on top of it. You know Aramus Randall, the old bushwhacker? A nigra, good with knives and guns, too."

Chris Colt was taking it all in. He picked up his glass and walked over to the bar and set his mug down next to the mountain man. "Couldn't help but overhear you, partner. Just wondering, who else runs with this Aramus?"

The mountain man gave Colt an appraising look and said, "Wal, lessee. The Clarkes. They're brothers or cousins or somethin'. Phineas and The Second Too-Tall Clarke. Both are rattlesnake mean. Too-Tall, I heerd he's killed two men with his bare hands, but they're both hellers with a gun. Lessee, there's another nigra runs with Aramus, kind of dumb boy. Don't know his name. I think Chink Church is runnin' with him, too. They ain't none of 'em worth two figs or a wrinkled-up pear. 'Cept I don't think I'll tell them to their faces. I'll just keep my opinions like that private amongst friends, you know."

Colt said, "This Chink Church. Is he half Chinese maybe?"

The man said, "That's him, awright. He'd stomp his mother into the ground to break in new hobnail boots, too. Real nice gent. He got bit by a buzztail last year and the snake died a half hour later."

The old man laughed at his own joke, and Colt signaled another shot for him and paid for it, having another beer himself, too.

" 'Bliged," the mountain man said. "Say, why you so curious?"

Colt said, "Just wondering. Fascinating stories going around, you know."

The man said, "Well, them Colts is fascinatin' that's for sure. Met ole Chris Colt one time. He was one fine man. Tough, too. Tougher'n the shoulder hide on a steel buffaler. Helped him out once in a little scrape down to Taos. Some yahoos tried to jump him in a saloon, was about a dozen of 'em. I took care of two of 'em and he done the rest, but he probly could a handled the two without my help."

Colt smiled at the bartender, saying, "Any man who would back a patriot like Chris Colt has my respect. Let me buy you a bottle. I insist."

The man beamed, "Well, thanks, stranger. It wasn't nothin' really."

The old man bit off a chew of tobacco, offering some to Colt, but he shook it off, lighting up a cigar instead.

Colt said, "Mister, you happen to know where any of them are now?"

The mountain man said, "Well, I heard ole Too-Tall Clarke got into another big brawl down in Trinidad and was headin' either to New Mexico or Texas. Don't know about the rest of 'em. Clarke was pretty cut up, I heard. Someone even said he got in a knife fight with Chris Colt's little boy and the kid stabbed him, but that's going a little too far with a story. Don't you think?"

Colt chuckled, saying, "I'd say so."

The old man said, "How come you want to know all that, mister?"

Chris said, "Told you. It's just interesting. I gotta go. See you."

Chris clapped the man in the shoulder and nodded at the grinning bartender, who winked.

The old man said, "Thanks for the whiskey, bub."

Chris Colt left the saloon, and the mountain man said, "Boy he was a curious sort. Never seen him afore. He a local?"

The bartender said, "Nope."

The old man took a sip of whiskey and shook his shoulders as it went down his throat. He said, "What was his name?"

The bartender polished a beer mug with a towel and calmly said, "Marshal Chris Colt."

The mountain man swallowed his wad of chewing tobacco and started coughing. A cowhand from Cortez standing near him started clapping him on the back.

By the time the man quit choking, Chris Colt had already booked himself and War Bonnet on a freight that would take him across LaVeta Pass. From there he would ride south to Trinidad, a relatively short distance. Chris headed to a general mercantile store near the train station and bought some new supplies. After that, he sent a telegram to Westcliffe, checked into a hotel, and bought a nice big supper.

Trinidad was one of the wildest towns in the West, and Chris Colt anticipated trouble whenever he went there. Now, however, he was visiting as a private citizen, not a U.S. marshal. Colt arrived after dark and checked into a boardinghouse on Main Street. Then he walked around until he found the busiest saloon in town and went in. There were cowhands, two professional gamblers, and a number of gun toughs. Colt heard murmurs as he passed through the batwing doors and bellied up to the bar. One young tough in the corner was swaggering like a rooster in a barnyard. Colt thought about leaving, because he knew by the murmurs that he had been recognized already. But he wanted to locate Too-Tall Clarke.

As Chris started to drink a cup of coffee, the young man sauntered over to the bar and flipped the fringe on Colt's war shirt.

The young gun tough apparently hadn't been told who Chris was.

He said, "Why you wearing the fancy buckskins and moccasins? You a red nigger lover or a scout or something?"

That he had too much to drink was quite obvious.

Colt said, "Yeah, or something."

The gunslinger said, "You a smart-ass?"

Colt said, "Nope, just trying to mind my own business."

The tough, still prodding, said, "Yeah, well, why ya drinking coffee? You a dandy that can't handle a man's drink?"

Colt still wouldn't look at the man and said, "Yes, that's right. Just wanted a quiet cup of coffee."

The gunslinger was getting upset because he wasn't getting a rise out of Colt. "Fancy Peacemakers you're wearing. Can you use 'em?"

Colt said, "A little bit, but I don't like to shoot much. Just consider a gun a tool."

The gunslinger was getting even more angry, because he was being stopped at every prod.

He said, "What are you, yellow?"

Colt calmly replied, "I hope not. Maybe."

The gunslinger came back, "I think you are."

Colt didn't say anything.

The young big-mouth said louder, "I said I think yer yellow."

Colt said, "Okay. You're allowed an opinion, sir."

The youngster said, "You never answered me about them clothes. Where d'you get that shirt?"

He actually admired the white buckskin war shirt with intricate-colored porcupine quill work, bead work, and long fringe, as well as silver concho shells.

Colt said, "A friend of mine."

The tough said, "Yeah, who?"

Colt took a sip of coffee and said, "Crazy Horse."

Before the gunslinger could respond, there was a scream from the back of the saloon and everyone looked. One of the bar women was standing near the piano, screaming at a rat running across the back of the saloon. A gun boomed before anybody could hardly move, and the rat disappeared.

The gunslinger turned his head and looked at

Chris Colt, who had just drawn and fired. Then Colt did a border shift, tossing his left-hand gun to his right while flipping the right-hand gun in the air and catching it with his left. Colt then spun both guns forward very rapidly, stopped them, and spun them backward, then forward and back into the twin engraved holsters. Colt then drew the left-hand gun with the speed of light, with the barrel pointing at the gun tough.

Colt ejected the empty shell and replaced it with one from his gun belt, explaining, "Whoops. Almost forgot to replace my spent shell. Like I said, just use guns as tools. You know, get rid of pests, things like that."

The gunslinger was ashen-faced. He turned and walked back to the back of the bar.

Colt picked up his cup and looked at the grinning bartender, who said, "I say, Constable Colt. You certainly handled that situation with dispatch."

Colt smiled, saying, "London?"

The man said, "No, Portsmouth. On the Channel, you know."

Chris Colt did not ask why a proper-speaking Englishman was tending bar in a rough saloon in Trinidad, Colorado. The West was not like that. Ex-lawyers had become wagon train scouts, librarians turned into outlaws, ex-Confederate generals were privates in the army, and so on. Many people left other lives behind to go West.

Colt said, "Good coffee. Looking for a tall fellow. Likes to fight."

The barkeep said, "Too-Tall Clarke, seven-foot-tall gentleman if he's an inch, and I use the term gentleman advisedly, I must say."

Colt said, "That's the one. Got a brother."

The bartender said, "Cousin, named Phineas. Trifle disagreeable gent. Too-Tall is simply evil. Put that hole in the back wall."

Colt looked at the back wall and saw where several boards had been nailed over a large hole.

Colt asked, "How did he do that?"

The bartender said, "He threw an unfortunate gent through it, I'm afraid."

Colt said, "You know where he might be right now, and his cousin?"

The bartender said, "He said he was going to Taos. Left this morning. Phineas, I presume, is creating mischief somewhere decent people would just like peace and quiet. I have no idea where the chap is these days."

Colt said, "Thanks, John."

The bartender said, "John?"

Colt smiled and said, "John Bull," and dropped a coin on the bar. "Keep the change."

The bartender chuckled and gave Colt a wave.

Chris noticed the young gunslinger seated by himself pouting and nursing a mug of beer in the back of the saloon. He shook his head as he walked down the street.

The next morning, Chris boarded another freight for Santa Fe. From there he and War Bonnet would make the familiar ride north to Taos. Colt spent another night in Santa Fe to let War Bonnet rest up. He had been working hard and still had hundreds of miles ahead of him.

The first view of Taos when traveling from the south was one of Chris Colt's favorite sights. Directly to his front was nestled the sleepy little town of Taos with pinion, cedar, and pine-covered mountains swirling around behind like a protective green shawl. To his left lay a long, giant green valley floor and cutting all the way through its center was a giant slash, wide in some places, narrow in others but always very deep. Like a jagged tear in the valley floor, this canyon held the winding, churning Rio Grande in its bottom. From here Colt could see only the top part of the sheer rock cliffs which towered over the canyon.

Too-Tall Clarke knew he was coming. A man who always had to duck when entering doors, a man who was equally good with guns or fists,

Too-Tall had spent time in Taos and had outlaw friends there. Chris Colt was a man that no outlaw wanted on his trail, and there was a sort of brotherhood amongst these men. They would help each other, because it would end up benefiting themselves. All would be happy to kill the legendary gunfighter, scout, and lawman.

Chris Colt was a man on a mission, and the word was out that he was hunting down the killers, one by one. His mission was even gossiped about in Westcliffe when Charley Colt was shopping.

Too-Tall knew that Colt could and would follow him all over the West, so he decided to try to stop the lawman at Taos. To that end, the big man had enlisted a gang of seven men. They had been watching the two main coach roads coming into Taos, one from the north and the other from the south. Both groups were on the high ground, waiting to shoot Colt from ambush, and would immediately send up a smoke signal if their ambush did not succeed. If it did succeed, they would send up two smoke signals, side by side. On a hunch, Too-Tall was with three of the men watching the southern road the day Chris Colt rode toward town.

When Colt was a short distance away, Too-Tall and his men were alerted by a man sent up on higher ground to alert them every time a traveler was spotted coming along a road. He was a half-breed simply known as Joe, who was half black and half Navajo. The men took their ambush positions. The plan was simple. They were hiding among rocks overlooking the trail at a narrow point. They would, when Colt came into the killing zone, wait for Too-Tall to fire the first shot and then open up themselves. The only part that Clarke worried about was that the spot they had picked was on a cliffside overlooking the rapids down below. If he missed with the first shot, Colt could clear the saddle and dive over the edge. Though it was hard to imagine he could survive, Too-Tall did not want to leave anything to chance. To make sure, Too-Tall roped a lightning-struck cedar tree and dragged it across the trail. This dead tree would force Colt to walk around it, away from the cliff and closer to the guns.

Joe came down the hillside, eyes open wide. He slid to a stop in front of Too-Tall, saying, "Big man, buckskins comes. He rides big paint with coup stripes and feathers in his mane and tail."

Too-Tall's heart pounded in his throat. He said, "That's Colt. Hide quick and get a round in your chamber."

Joe scrambled off to the uphill side and hid behind a large rock. Too-Tall gave hand signals to each man to keep quiet and get ready.

Chris Colt was about to round the bend in the trail, and as he always did on a trail, he visualized what lay ahead. He was always alert to likely ambush locations. As he remembered, the trail narrowed and ran along a cliff overlooking the Rio Grande a hundred feet below. It was an excellent ambush spot, so he would out of habit approach with extreme care.

The other precaution Colt took was to always keep an eye on War Bonnet's ears. The big horse had a much better nose than Colt and very large ears that could turn in any direction. When Joe scrambled down the hill, Chris Colt could not hear him, but War Bonnet did. His ears picked up the sounds of the pebbles being stirred and rolling downhill. It was a danger sound, and his ears instinctively turned forward, his neck stretched out, and his nostrils flared in and out, testing the wind for bad smells. His rider noticed and immediately reined his horse in to assess the situation.

Five minutes passed, and Too-Tall Clarke, hiding behind a thick tree trunk, squinted his eyes, straining to see his target coming into view. He heard the metallic clink of a horse's hooves and saw the head of War Bonnet coming around the bend. He squinted across the V in his back sight. But there was no rider in the saddle.

Too-Tall heard the distinctive cocking of two pistols behind him, up the hill. He spun around to see Chris Colt, a cigarillo between his teeth and a Colt Peacemaker in each hand. The left one pointed at Too-Tall and the second one pointed at Joe.

Colt said, "Well, boys, you wanted a party, huh? Well, I'm ready to dance. You Too-Tall Clarke?"

Too-Tall gulped and said, "Yeah."

Colt said, "One shot from any of your boys and you take a gut shot. I'll take several with me, maybe all of you." Yelling, he said, "You all hear that? Drop the iron, or you won't be getting paid, and some of you will be moving to Boot Hill! Raise your hands and walk out here with Clarke."

Joe did not respect, or maybe understand, Colt's reputation as much as the others. Colt saw it in the man's eyes before Joe even tried to swing the gun. Chris already had his right-hand Colt pointed at Joe, and he only needed to squeeze the trigger. He put two shots in the man's heart, holes that could have been covered with a quarter, and the half-breed slumped to the ground.

Colt said, "Anybody else feel lucky?"

The men quickly walked down to Too-Tall, their hands held high. Colt motioned them all together in a group with his guns.

He commanded, "Turn around and let me look for hideouts, boys."

They all spun around slowly in a circle.

Colt then said, "Have a seat."

They sat down, and he slowly walked around, picking up guns and tossing them over the cliff into the river. Colt sat down on a log and held his left gun on Clarke, saying, "You attacked my family. That's declaring war on me and mine. I'll ask one time only. Who stabbed my wife?"

Colt already knew it was Aramus, but he wanted to start with a few questions he already knew the answers to. That way, if Too-Tall told the truth on those questions Colt could assume he was getting accurate information.

Fighting the fear that was paralyzing him, Too-Tall didn't answer. If there was only some way out of this . . .

Chris said, "Too slow."

The left-hand gun boomed, and Too-Tall Clarke fell to the ground, screaming in pain and clutching his right knee with both hands. Blood ran between his fingers as the tall man moaned and writhed on the ground.

Chris said, "Now, I can keep it up. They're going to have to change your name to Too-Short Clarke. We can do this easy or we can do this hard. Don't forget, I've lived with the Lakotah and the Cheyenne. No matter what happens, one way or another, you will tell me what I want to know before you die. Now, who stabbed my wife?"

Clarke said, "Aramus Randall. Nigra fella. Mean and tough as blazes with a blade."

Colt said, "Tough with women." He spat on the ground in disgust. "You can take off your scarf and bind up your knee."

Clarke meekly said, "Obliged, Marshal."

Colt corrected him, "I'm not a marshal now. I'm a man at war with those who attacked my family."

Chris knew he had Clarke now, and he questioned him to get ideas where he might locate the others.

Unfortunately, Chris Colt did not know about the other gang guarding the northern route into Taos. Nor did he know about Ribs Bracken, a two-bit outlaw who went back and forth between Colorado and New Mexico pulling petty robberies from time-to-time. He had seen Colt in the Trinidad saloon and was recognized by one of the gang members as he headed down the road to Taos from the north. Once they heard the news, the gang galloped through Taos toward the southern gang's ambush location.

Chris said, "Boys, I don't know what he promised you to help him, but my fight's with him and his amigos. I'll give each of you an opportunity you don't deserve. I hear the weather's warm down in Mexico. If you want to cut and run that way, I'll allow it. The deal, though, is this: if you leave, the next time I see you, any of you, I'll pull iron without a warning and shoot you on sight. You'll have the same opportunity on me."

Chris should have looked over at War Bonnet's ears while he was talking, because the big paint had stopped cropping bunchgrass and was staring down the trail.

Too late Colt heard a gun click, then the sound of men approaching from behind.

One of the outlaws behind him said, "Thet's real white of ya, but Ah jest cain't see us lettin' you go like thet. Right, boys?"

Colt heard the laughs and chuckles behind him and counted four men. He dropped his guns and raised his hands.

Too-Tall, with a big smile on his face, struggled to his feet, saying, "Somebody untie me quicklike."

The four outlaws came down and one retrieved Colt's guns and his bowie knife on his gun belt, but they didn't notice the one strapped to the middle of his back. That gave Colt some hope. All four were grinning as Too-Tall was untied, and he hopped forward to Chris Colt. He raised a .44 and swung it viciously at Colt's face. Colt ducked his head back and the pistol swept by in front of his nose. The momentum threw Too-Tall off balance and unceremoniously onto his rear end, to the laughter of his compadres.

Teeth clenched in rage and severe pain, he struggled up on his good leg and pointed the .44 at Colt's face. As he cocked it, Chris Colt spat at him.

Too-Tall grinned sadistically, saying, "Just like yer old lady, huh, Colt. Wal, let's see you dodge this."

Everyone heard the swooshing sound. In the next moment the turkey feathers of an Apache arrow stuck out of the center of Too-Tall's chest. Colt reacted instantly. He grabbed the dying man's .44 and started fanning shots at the other outlaws. At the same time the hillside behind him exploded in bullets. The outlaws dropped like an avalanche had hit them. Too-Tall still stood bolt upright, staring in shock at the protruding arrow.

Colt, having run out of his six bullets, looked around as twenty Jicarilla Apaches came down the hillside, wielding smoking rifles. He saw a familiar sight as Man Killer's big black Appaloosa came bounding over the hilltop and down the ridge, but the rider was not his young Nez Percé protégé. It was his beautiful sister, Charley Colt.

She rode up to Chris and said, "You okay?"

Colt smiled and nodded.

Charlotte Colt was not in a friendly mood. She looked at Too-Tall and said, "You Too-Tall Clarke?"

Dumbfounded and in shock, he meekly nodded. Charley tossed him her left-hand gun. Amazingly, he caught it.

She said, "You helped kill my sister-in-law. Use it!"

He looked at the gun in his hand, and thought to himself, She's just a girl. A big smile crossed his face, as his thumb went over the hammer to cock the little Navy .36. As he started to raise it, though, he saw her right hand flash down and smoothly draw, cock, and fire her other gun. He felt the bullet slam into his chest and he toppled back off the cliff and out into midair. Down, down he fell, and when he hit the river, the force of the fall snapped his spine in two places. His limp body was carried down the rapids and away.

Charley said, "Any more of them in the gang?"

Chris said, "No Charley, how the hell did you get here? What are you doing?"

Charlotte grinned, saying, "How did I get with these Apaches?"

Colt nodded, still amazed at his sister.

She said, "Well, you probably hadn't even left Trinidad before the word was all around that you were coming here first after Too-Tall Clarke. I lived with the Jicarilla, remember. I figured you might need some help. We followed those four here."

She indicated the four newest gang members lying dead in front of them. While she and Chris talked, the Apaches approached the gang members who were still tied.

One of them, in a panic, said, "Mr. Colt. I was going to take you up on your offer about Mexico, sir."

Then man next to him chimed in, "Me, too, Marshal."

The one next to him said the same, as did the one on the end.

Colt smiled and said, "I don't know, boys. What you did sure wasn't very friendly. Can you all swim?"

They got very nervous then and Colt retrieved his guns and knife, then untied them all.

Chris looked at his sister and smiled and told them, "Take off your boots."

Remembering what happened to Too-Tall, they did not hesitate.

Gesturing with his gun, Colt said, "Now your drawers and your shirts."

They again complied quickly while Charley and the Apaches started laughing.

Colt pointed south and said, "Mexico's that direction. Don't worry, the Apaches here will take good care of your horses. These braves look very hungry to me."

Clad only in long johns, the would-be killers quickly headed south on the trail, feeling lucky to still have their scalps attached.

Chris Colt was introduced to the Jicarillas, and he offered them all the clothing, horses, and equipment left behind by the outlaws. In the meantime, he poured coffee for himself and his sister, and they sat down on the log.

Chris said, "Thanks, sister. You saved my

bacon." He smiled and leaned over, kissing Charley on the forehead.

He said, "What about the children?"

Charlotte said, "They're fine. About half of Custer and Fremont county are around them all the time now wanting to protect them. I heard you were headed here, so I came down with great haste and got my old friends here to help me out."

Colt smiled, a far-off look on his face.

Charley said, "So where you headed?"

Chris said, "Texas. Too-Tall's cousin is holding up stages there from what he told me. He's next, I guess."

She said, "Well, let's try to keep this trip a little more quiet, so they don't greet you the same way when you arrive."

Colt smiled. "Well, I'm not worried if they do. My little sister will come and save my worthless hide."

Colt moved east out of Santa Fe and headed for the Llano Estacado, the Staked Plain of the Texas panhandle. The Staked Plain was a harsh, unforgiving land and a dangerous place for a man to travel if he did not know what he was doing.

In Amarillo, Colt started hearing news. A

group of bandits had been holding up stages all over the western portion of Texas, and although they wore bandannas during hold-ups, those who knew him were positive that the leader of the gang was Phineas Clarke.

Heading south toward the Rio Grande, Colt stopped in at a stage stop saloon not far from Big Spring and Sweetwater and learned that most of the stage attacks had been occurring in that area. The outlaws' general method of robbery was to pick a place near the highest point in a long grade, where the stage horses would be going their slowest. If the holdup men could find good cover near that spot, they would pop out, each brandishing, of all things, a Colt revolving shotgun. According to all reports there was a total of five men.

He caught up with them twenty miles outside of Sweetwater, alerted by gunshots. A passenger inside the big Concord stagecoach that day was a former Pinkerton agent who had also worked as a deputy marshal in a small town in eastern Kansas. He was now traveling around as a drummer, selling Smith & Wesson firearms to mercantile stores all over the West. He considered himself a westerner and would not succumb to intimidation. He was carrying a matched pair of engraved Smith & Wesson American

.44's. The pistols, with ivory grips, scroll engraving, and silver plating were good shooting firearms. The problem, however, was his decision to use them against five Colt revolving shotguns.

Phineas was a gunfighter, and when he assessed the people inside the stage, he immediately picked up the man's intentions by his giveaway looks and the set of his jaw. The drummer was steeling himself to the challenge before him. He could not see under the outlaw's mask, because if he had he would have seen a big grin spreading across the face of Phineas Clarke.

His hands streaked down for his .44's. He felt hope when he cleared leather, but Phineas instantly aimed his shotgun. When the drummer saw the shotgun leveled at him, the man tried to turn his guns, but it was too late. The giant revolver roared. A melon-sized hole appeared in the side of the Concord, right below the drummer's face, chest, and shoulders. The gun salesman's body was flung backward and slammed against the man next to him. The shotgun roared again, and the left half of the drummer's neck disappeared, his head falling over sideways and hanging on his shoulder. Two women in the Concord screamed, and all the passengers dived on top of each other, trying to lie on the floor.

Two of them had a pellet each in their left shoulders from Phineas's double-ought buckshot.

From his vantage point some three miles distant, Chris Colt heard the reports and saw the puffs of smoke from the shotgun. He quickly kicked sand over the smokeless, dry-wood cooking fire he'd made and poured the contents of his coffeepot over it. He threw his equipment in his saddlebags, rolled his bedroll, and tied it behind his saddle.

Chris whistled and said, "War Bonnet, come here, boy," and the big paint trotted up to him.

Colt threw the saddle on his back. He ran the cinch under the chest and tightened it up, still hurrying, but then, standing in front of the horse, he carefully pulled each foreleg forward to ensure that the skin was not cinched under the tight leather strap.

"Time to go to work, buddy," he said as he vaulted into the saddle.

Checking his guns while he rode, Colt took off toward the holdup at a fast trot. It was foolish to run full-out trying to get to the scene. His horse would be wiped out before he even arrived. He might have a long ride in front of him, Colt thought, and War Bonnet had a mile-eating walk as it was. He also had a slow trot which

Colt just loved. The big horse enjoyed that slow trot, and could keep going all day with it.

Phineas spotted Colt when he was still over a mile off. "All right, we gotta git goin'!" He gave his men the signal to head out. They took off across the prairie at a dead run, not looking back.

Colt stopped at the Concord stage. He was very upset by what he found. The drummer and the driver were dead. Colt heard moaning and found the express guard lying in the floor board of the driver's compartment with part of his left forearm shot away and a bad cut across his right cheekbone. None of the passengers were westerners and were all in shock, three men and two women. On top of that, one of the women and one man had been shot in their shoulders.

Chris Colt was torn between tending to their wounds and chasing the outlaws. They no doubt had good mounts. One of the ways Colt and other lawmen spotted outlaws was by checking their horses. When some hardcases came into a lawman's town, they might just be tough cowboys from a rough ranch, but if they had cheap clothes, cheap saddles, cheap everything but outstanding horses, they were usually outlaws. The horses were always needed for the getaway.

In the end, Colt just could not leave the wounded passengers unattended. He dismounted and determined which wounds were the most severe. He yanked the petticoat off a very shocked older woman and immediately tore it into strips. The expressman's arm was bleeding profusely. Colt took three of the man's bullets from his gun belt and piled them on top of the wound and bound them tightly with a strip of cloth. This put direct pressure on the wound and stopped the bleeding. Chris discovered that the man's forearm was not only broken but several inches of the radial bone had been shot away. Colt first bandaged the exposed flesh, then tied four sticks placed around the forearm, making a tight splint. Chris felt that he had the bones lined up pretty well, so maybe, just maybe, a good doctor would be able to save the arm.

Colt then started a fire and had the healthy passengers gather more wood to burn in the fire. He put his coffeepot on the fire and stuck the tip of his bowie in the hottest part of the flames. Colt checked out the shoulder wounds of the two passengers but could tell little. The pellets had gone through the woman's shoulder. Those in the man, though, were wedged somewhere inside his beefy shoulder. Chris decided to cauterize both shoulder wounds as best he could, then bandage them. Later a doctor would have to remove the buckshot.

When Chris Colt used the red-hot point of the bowie knife, he almost had to laugh. The woman acted bravely and gritted her teeth together, even though she had tears streaming down her cheeks. The man, on the other hand, screamed like a two-year-old and had to be held down by the other passengers.

Chris found some cups in the boot and poured coffee for the passengers. He was going to head out, but they begged him to stay until they could get help. No one wanted to remain in that wasteland unprotected. To make matters worse, Chris Colt heard behind him the rumblings of far-off thunder. Turning, he saw a monster storm that was headed their way. With the warm weather and the size and shape of the thunderheads, it looked like the type that could spawn a Texas twister.

Chris Colt was said to be able to track a memory back through time after five full years. He was so adept at trailing, it was said, he could follow the trail of a thistledown blowing through mountain passes. Unfortunately, Chris Colt knew by the speed and the severity of the approaching storm that he was going to lose all chance of tracking the outlaws.

*   *   *

When he was finally able to hail a stage heading into Sweetwater, Chris sent a telegram to his cousin, Justis Colt, about the gang of cutthroats. Colt was then forced to take a room and stay there for three days, as a series of storms and several cyclones pounded the area. Colt waited by the window as any chance of tracking the outlaws was washed away.

On the third day, though, luck came his way. He was handed a telegram from Justis. His cousin said he had reports of a gang who had just appeared in southeastern Kansas to rob a stage.

Chris Colt headed north the next morning. He would chase Phineas Clarke all over Kansas if need be. Colt laid over in Wichita and headed toward Salina the next day. After two weeks, with twelve of those nights sleeping under the stars, Chris finally got another strong lead on the Clarke gang. They had worked their way northward from Dodge City, pulling two jobs outside Hays, and seemed to be now heading back toward him.

A few days later, a stage was held up outside Topeka, and Chris Colt headed that way as quickly as possible. He visited with the marshal there and saw the telegram that came in that a gang of road agents had held up a stage outside Emporia, armed with Colt revolving shotguns.

Colt preferred the eastern side of the state because of its gullies, trees, and hills. Out west toward Colorado, the land was as flat as a tabletop. It was advantageous in pursing criminals in that he could sometimes see the outlaws when they were miles away, but that was a disadvantage, too, in that the outlaws could see the pursuers and always know the status of the chase.

That was exactly Phineas Clarke's plan. By now he had heard Chris Colt was pursuing him. Clarke headed west across the hundreds of miles of flat, open prairie, where prairie grasses waved in the wind like ocean waves on a rolling sea.

In Dodge City, Phineas and his men bought supplies, including tarpaulins, miner's picks, and shovels. They headed out west, not attempting to hide their trail. Phineas Clarke wanted Colt to follow him.

Chris Colt arrived in Dodge City soon after. Picking up as much as he could on the gang, he discovered from the mercantile owner that they had bought picks and shovels and a large tarpaulin made of oil cloth. Colt made the same assumption any other thinking lawman would have made: These men were going to dig a large hole, wrap their loot in oil cloth, and bury it until things cooled down.

Phineas was meticulous in his preparations. The men in his gang carefully cut clumps of sod out of the prairie grass and set them aside while each dug a hole. The dirt from each hole was carefully shoveled into each man's sandbag to equal their weight in the saddle. Then strips of tarpaulin were cut large enough to cover each man's hole. Phineas took one of the saddlebags full of money and one of the Colt shotguns and dropped them on the trail. Tracks were carefully smoothed over, and one man was selected to take the horses in one line, tails tied to the reins of the horse trailing, and keep heading on to Colorado.

Hours passed. The men smoked and shouted back and forth to each other. A herd of pronghorn showed on the horizon, and at Phineas's instructions they all hid in their holes until the antelope passed between them, heading toward a distant water hole. When Clarke gave the signal, the men sat on the edge of their holes and Phineas told them how great it was that the antelope did not even spook at their scent when the herd passed by. He felt certain if the sharp-sighted beast did not detect the men, the mighty Chris Colt would not.

At long last, one of the men gave the signal, and they looked far to the east, where a dot appeared on the horizon. Two of the smokers extinguished their cigarettes. Each man took a drink of water from his canteen and checked the loads in his rifle. As the dot started taking the shape of a buckskin-clad man on a black-and-white paint, they slid under their tarpaulins, placing their sod lids in place. The grass was high enough here that the men did not really have to be completely covered, but Phineas Clarke would take no chances. Chris Colt had escaped too many ambushes in his life.

Colt saw the saddlebags and shotgun on the ground long before he got to them, and it immediately put him on his guard. His eyes scoured the tall grass in circles all the way around him. He would look up close, then his eyes would move out a little and check all the way around again. Why, he wondered, would the bags and gun have been dropped?

Before he dismounted, he looked carefully at War Bonnet's ears, waiting for any sign of danger. The big horse was nervous but not alarmed yet. Colt took one last look around before getting down. It seemed safe.

As he bent to pick up the saddlebags, the men behind him sat up in their holes, off to both his

left and right rear. He didn't see the outlaws,
only War Bonnet's sudden alarm as the big
horse got a scent of two of them. Colt drew both
Peacemakers and started to whirl around, but it
was too late. He saw flames coming at him and
got off a shot at one of them before he went
down under a hail of bullets.

CHAPTER 7

Survive!

Rain was pouring down, and the darkness was lit by frequent flashes of lightning. The cold driving rain made Chris Colt's eyes flutter open. He had no idea where he was or what was happening. Then lightning crashed particularly close on the plain nearby, and Colt remembered. He had been bushwhacked. Everything went black again.

Something sharp tore into Colt's upper leg and his eyes opened with a start. A coyote had Chris Colt's quadriceps in his teeth and Colt screamed at the animal. He jumped back and yelped and the other three coyotes with it ran out of sight into the prairie grass. They were not sure if this prey was dead or alive, but now they knew.

Colt blinked his eyes against the hot sun and looked down. The ground all about was wet and muddy. He discovered that he was staked out, spread-eagle fashion. He was covered in blood and was completely naked. As he became more awake, Chris started feeling sharp pain from bullet wounds. His stomach growled from tremendous hunger and thirst. It was coming back to him now. Colt got angry with himself for allowing himself to get suckered like he did, but he could not afford to remain angry. The hunger helped him think more clearly. It suddenly dawned on him; the shovels, and picks, the tarp. Phineas Clarke hadn't been burying loot. He'd been burying himself and his men so they could set up their ambush. Chris Colt made up his mind right then. He would survive. He would hunt down the men who did this to him, and make them pay.

With that thought, his mind became clear as a bell. First, he had to decide how badly he was wounded. The severe pain in his back told him they must have used rifles. He felt a wound in his left shoulder and one just below his right shoulder. One had grazed his ribs on the right side, because it hurt to breathe. He looked down and saw the exit holes in his upper chest where the two through his shoulders had come through cleanly, without the bullets mushrooming. Colt figured that happened because the men were so close when they shot him, maybe no more than twenty paces away. He recalled four guns firing before he blacked out, and he was sure he had got one of them with a snap shot. Another bullet had torn across his abdominal muscles when he was turning. A bullet had hit his left triceps muscle from behind, but it didn't feel like the bone was hit. Both legs felt like there might be several bullets in each, all from behind.

A wave of terrible fear swept over him, and he started to cry. Several minutes passed before he could stop himself.

Speaking out loud, Colt said to himself, "All right, Chris, you've had your cry. Now it's time to think. You've been through almost as bad, and you'll make it this time."

Feeling more hopeful, Colt looked up at the cloudless sky that stretched endlessly to the far horizons. "God, thanks for letting me live this far. If you call me up there, please reunite me with Shirley, forever. If not, please help me hunt down all of them. Give me strength. In Jesus's name, Amen."

He looked down at his blood-caked body and tried to survey his wounds. He spotted two holes where bullets had passed through each thigh, again without mushrooming and creating a large exit hole.

Colt then remembered coming to during the big thunderstorm and realized just how things work out. The severe thunderstorm had actually saved his life. The rain had washed out his many wounds, and the mud underneath had plugged up the bullet holes.

Gritting his teeth, Colt decided he would see if the rain had loosened the stakes his arms and legs were tied to. Wincing in pain, he pulled on each stake individually, until he finally felt a little give with the one next to his right wrist. Patiently, for what seemed like hours, Chris pulled and wiggled the stake. Twice he passed out from the excruciating pain.

Finally, it loosened enough that he could pull it free. Chris cried again, this time in relief. He started laughing, first softly and then hysterically. The laughter turned into tears, then back into laughter.

Colt slowly, fighting off the fierce pain, removed the bonds one by one. Carefully he shook his limbs until the circulation returned. He then looked around for tracks but found nothing. The rains had washed out everything.

Colt grabbed all four stakes—he'd chew off the leather bonds, later—and dug into the mud with a stake. Gradually he made a bowl in the ground and watched the water from the mud seep into it. He stuck his face down into the bowl and drank deeply until the brown liquid was gone. Colt waited for more water to seep in and drank again. He did this over and over until his thirst was sated.

Chris thought to locate the holes where the men had hidden. Maybe he'd find something he could use for survival. He tried to stand, but realized then that both legs had been broken by bullets. Colt dragged himself to where he guessed the holes must be. He fainted twice more from the effort, but then scolded himself that he could not afford to faint anymore or he would perish. Not until nightfall, did he find the second one where he spotted a piece of tarp that had been left. He crawled into the hole and wrapped himself up and slept.

When Chris Colt awakened, the morning sun was already an hour into the sky. His stomach felt like his throat had been slit, and he knew he had to find water and get food. A movement caught his eye, and Colt saw a herd of prong-horn moving toward him. He lay flat and waited. The herd passed nearby, heading for a waterhole in the distance. Chris Colt wasted no time. Crawling after them, he made sure he kept their tracks in front of him. Progress was agonizingly slow, and he still hadn't seen anything by the time he finally fell asleep that night.

The next morning, he continued crawling, putting one arm ahead of the other. He was encouraged by the sight of several bumblebees flying overhead, knowing they were headed for water. Colt laughed at himself when he finally looked up and saw a grove of cottonwoods not two hundred yards away.

Chris made it to the trees and found a small stream passing among them. He stuck his head underwater and shook out the cobwebs. Then he drank for a long time. He had the tarp wrapped around him and tied it around his waist with one of the leather thongs.

Crawling away from the water, Colt found a campsite far enough off that he would not disturb the animals that regularly came to the creek to drink. Next, he crawled to several of the trees and started gathering firewood. Using two of the leather thongs, he bent down a branch, making a crude snare. He had no bait, so he made one thong into a noose and placed it across a little trail in the underbrush leading to the creek. Chris crawled back to his campsite and waited.

He saw a coyote come up to drink and two mule deer. Neither saw him but acted nervous smelling his scent in the area. Right before dark

Colt heard a slight squeal. He slowly made his way to the snare, and tears flooded his eyes as he saw a small rabbit hanging limply from his noose. Colt released the rabbit and carefully cradled it as he slowly crawled back to his hiding place. Having no other implements, he bit the stomach fur open and stuck his fingers in the hole. Peeling the skin away in both directions, he tore the skin from the flesh all the way from the head to the hindlegs. He next pulled the flesh apart, exposing the intestines. Chris grabbed the head and forelegs in one hand and the hindlegs in the other. He raised the rabbit and jerked down, and the entrails flew out onto the ground. Colt reached inside and scraped the residue out with his fingers. Finally, he grabbed the head and twisted it around in a tightening circle until it tore off.

Colt tossed it away, then crawled to the creek and washed the rabbit out thoroughly. He bit into the hindquarters and tore away a chunk of meat. Colt gnawed hungrily on the uncooked flesh, savoring every bite. At the end he licked his fingers, then crawled to the stream and drank. Water had never tasted so good.

He needed a knife, though. He searched the banks of the little waterway for stones he could use. He finally found one that had sharp edges, almost resembling a spearhead. With that and several other stones he returned to his little campsite.

Using his makeshift knife, Colt took off the tarpaulin and made a neck hole in it. He put it back on like a poncho and tied the thong around his waist. He then started scraping the inside of the rabbit's fur. The fur was actually comprised of two pieces and they were very small, but maybe they could be used for something. Next he found a dry, flat piece of wood and used the point of the rock to wedge out a small hole. He got a small but stout green stick and tied a thong to it at both ends like a bow. Colt then grabbed one of the rocks he had gotten earlier, one that was rounded on one side and flat on the other. So far, so good.

Colt collected a small pile of tinder and put it all around the flat wood. Around a dry stick with a pointed end, about a foot and half long, he wrapped the thong, holding the rounded part of the rock with the flat side pushing down on the stick. The pointed end of the stick was placed in the hole started in the flat board. Then moving the bow back and forth, the thong wrapped around the stick made it spin rapidly like a drill, first one direction and then the other. Aching from the exertion, Colt spun the stick back and forth until he finally saw a small puff of smoke emerge from the little hole in the wood. He spun it even faster, and soon more smoke came out, then a slight spark. Excited, Colt started blowing on the tinder. A little flame popped up and ignited the little pile of tinder. He added firewood and soon a small flame was licking upward. It became bigger as Colt fed thicker sticks, then small logs onto the fire. Chris Colt smiled. He would not freeze this night

Coals remained from the fire when he awakened at dawn. Colt knew he had a large task before him this day. Quickly he worked on the point of the longest stake with his spear-point rock. He sharpened the stake as much as he could, then removed his poncho. He'd have to be naked when he made his kill.

Armed, Colt crawled back to the creek where the animals came to drink. Fighting off the morning chill, he waited until at last he saw what he wanted. He slipped into the stream and waited.

The herd of pronghorn showed up on the vast prairie beyond. They grazed forward cautiously, noses testing the wind. As they drew close, their eyes peered in among the trees for any signs of natural enemies. Finally satisfied that their favorite watering hole was safe, the antelope carefully moved into the trees. One by one they started drinking at the little stream. One of the last ones was a doe, leaning over in the ideal spot for Colt's plan.

A tanned hand shot out of the water, followed instantly by another that jabbed the stake into the left side of the animal's chest. The pronghorn let out a loud bleat like a frightened lamb, and the others fled, dashing out of sight. The pronghorn tried to pull back in sheer panic and pain, but Chris's grip was like iron. He held on to the kicking and thrashing animal until its strength waned. At last it stopped moving altogether. Colt set the body on his back and crawled back to his nearby camp. The lawman built up the fire and blew on the coals to ignite the wood. Then he started dressing out the animal. When he finished, he was exhausted, and he had to lie down and nap for a couple of hours. After he awakened, Colt gathered some wild turnips and other plants he had seen earlier, preparing them with two large antelope steaks. He was going to have himself a feast.

After eating, Chris cut strips off the bottom of the tarpaulin and stuck his right foot in the fork of a double-trunked tree. He then used sticks and tied the strips around his leg, making a splint. Even if he couldn't walk, he wanted to insure that the bones healed together properly.

Colt finished the afternoon, after a short nap, by concentrating on taking care of his wounds. He used the creek as a mirror to check the ones he had trouble seeing. Sure enough, the rainstorm really had been his savior. Nowhere could he see or feel any telltale pus that indicated an infection.

Colt could not keep his eyes open any longer, and he fell asleep making a poultice for one of his wounds from some leaves he had managed to gather. He was sleeping very soundly when his eyes suddenly popped open. Was that . . . ? There were snowflakes falling on his face. He opened his eyes wide and saw nothing but darkness. A few embers in his firepit gave off a faint red glow. Looking closer, he saw a puff of steam and a little hiss from a snowflake landing on it.

Colt shivered and said, "Damn, Colt, why didn't you make a lean-to first, idiot?"

He built the fire up, then crawled around with his sharp rock, sawing away at evergreen branches. He dragged them one by one to his campsite. He bent a sapling over, tying it down to a deadfall log with one of the thongs. He bent another over and tied it down, too, with a length cut off that thong. Then he started interweaving the evergreen boughs between the two saplings. By now there was more than a skiff of snow covering the ground out in the prairie, but the trees sheltered him somewhat.

Colt kept working on the shelter long into the night, because it was essential for him to get as warm as possible with just an oilcloth poncho for clothing. He had intended to stake the antelope hide out in the sun and tan it, but he hadn't been able to start on that.

By midnight, Colt felt satisfied and crawled into his shelter, which was a cross between a lean-to and an Apache wickiup, a lodge made of woven branches. Although he had started with the two bent-over saplings, he now had numerous branches cross-woven within each other, as well as logs and rocks holding them down on the ground so the wind could not blow away the structure. When he was done, he had three solid windproof walls, a roof, all sloping so water would run off, and an opening which faced the campfire, which was now covered, too. He would be plenty warm. Colt stoked the fire up and lay down to sleep.

It was after daybreak when Colt awakened. The snow had stopped, he saw. The ground was covered with about a foot of snow, and away from the trees, Colt saw swirled drifts even deeper.

Colt spent the morning treating his wounds and rebandaging. After that, he gathered some more firewood, knocking snow off each piece and crawling back through the snow and drying off and warming by the fire. He caught another rabbit in his snare, but this time it was a jackrabbit, and Colt was very excited. He would get enough fur and leather from that to make moccasins. He was also going to use the antelope hide to start making himself clothing.

He followed a similar routine for the next week. By that time Colt had a lot of his strength back, and though he could not walk, Colt did have enough hides to make himself an outfit, moccasins, and mittens. He's killed, skinned, and tanned three more rabbits. He had taken the hide of one rabbit and hung it up to attract a bobcat, coyote, or fox. The flapping skin hanging near the snare had made one antelope curious and attracted him close enough for Colt to spear it.

Colt had enough hide left over to make himself a backpack, and he washed out the bladders of the two antelopes and made them into canteens. Packing up with wild roots and herbs, beef jerky, dry tinder wrapped in oilcloth to

start fires easily, the bow firestarter, full canteens, and his handmade spear and knife, Chris
Colt set out. Several hundred miles of prairie
lay ahead of him, and the only people he might
encounter could be outlaws or unfriendly Indians. The major obstacle was that Chris Colt
would have to chase after the killers by drag-
ging himself along the ground on his belly.

By this time, Phineas Clarke and his gang
members were in a saloon back in Trinidad, Colorado. They had decided to return to the rough
town to let things cool down in Texas and Kansas. The biggest mistake they had made, though,
was bragging to every yahoo and want-to-be
gunslick they came across that they had killed
Chris Colt—except they left out the part about
backshooting him.

The men had just bellied up to the bar and
gotten drinks when the batwing doors swung
open. All of a sudden the place fell pin-drop
silent.

Phineas's jaw dropped. At first he thought he
was looking at Chris Colt, but the man was
black. Clarke did a double take, and then realized that he was looking at Joshua Colt, Chris's
older brother. Standing next to him was a handsome Indian, wearing double Colt Peacemakers.

Between them was one of the most beautiful young women Clarke had ever seen in his life. Yet along with long golden blond hair, hypnotic eyes, and high cheekbones, he noticed the twin Colt Navy .36's slung low in double hand-tooled holsters on her hips. This had to be Charley Colt.

Being a fighter, Clarke noticed something else. All three of them had their belt loops filled with extra bullets. That meant these three had come to fight.

Joshua looked at Clarke and said, "So you're the mighty Phineas Clarke. We've heard that you men have been bragging that you murdered our brother, Chris Colt, in Kansas. That right?"

Clarke was scared to death, so he did what he always did when he was frightened. He acted tough. It had always worked for him before.

He said, "Actually, Colt was alive when we left him west of Dodge City. He had a few dozen bullet holes, and his clothes, and horse, and gear was gone. Some nasty person even staked him out on the prairie, so he could go under proper."

Joshua said, "Well, friends, you chose the wrong man to shoot. Now you're all gonna die."

Sweat broke out on Clarke's upper lip.

Joshua's hand hovered over his guns while he

stared into Phineas's cold eyes, and he said, "This one's mine."

Charley said, "I'll take the ugly one on the right."

Man Killer said, "I'm just going to start shooting white men."

This unnerved the remaining two outlaws, and both went for their guns. Man Killer chose these two to kill. True to her word, Charley drew and fired two bullets into the chest of the ugly man. Joshua, his jaw set and teeth clenched, drew and fired as Phineas was still clearing leather.

His first bullet took the man above the belt buckle. Joshua stepped forward, still shooting, and said, "You shot my brother and brag about it." Then Joshua said, "And you helped kill my sister-in-law."

The outlaw was in shock that this man had outdrawn him. He knew Chris Colt was incredibly fast, but he didn't know about his brother.

Phineas Clarke, with two bullets in his belly, sat down in place, a dazed look on his face. But his gun was still in his hand, and he raised it. Man Killer, Charley, and Joshua each fanned a bullet into him simultaneously. The force of the three slugs in his chest drove his body back into a support post along the bar. His head dropped down on his chest, and his blank eyes stared at the floor. The ugly one, lying on the floor, moaned once, then gave out a wail. He moved once more and died. Charlotte looked at the carnage.

Charley said, "So much violence. So much killing. Will it ever end, Joshua?"

Joshua replied, "Yes. When men learn to live under the law and treat each other with dignity and respect."

Man Killer chuckled.

Puzzled, Charlotte said, "What's so funny?"

The Nez Percé responded, "Joshua now sounds like his brother speaking."

The thought struck her, and she chuckled, too. Then it struck a funny chord with Joshua, and he, too, laughed at himself, but after several seconds his laugh turned into a sob, which he stifled.

He hung his head, ashamed, muttering, "Sorry."

Man Killer said, "You both tried to hide from my words: I shall find Colt. He lives."

There was a long silence, then Joshua queried, "Are you sure? After all, my brother is still only a man."

Man Killer said confidently, "Do not worry. We have all just lost a sister, so we worry now about losing a brother. Maybe a warrior such as Wyatt Earp or Bat Masterson could have killed our brother, but men such as these could not kill the mighty Colt, not even from ambush. They might hurt him, for even a pack of coyotes might bite and hurt the great bear many times, but they could never kill him."

Charley said, "Why?"

Man Killer replied, "For they are lowly coyotes who eat only carrion and travel in packs, and he is a grizzly with much courage and power. His medicine is too strong. I will find Chris Colt and bring him home to his family. I have spoken."

CHAPTER 8
The Search

Chris Colt made camp the first night far west of his previous location, but looking back, he could see the tops of the trees where he had been. He found a buffalo wallow and crawled inside, then realized he didn't have firewood, except for what was in his pack. Leaving his pack, he hobbled out of the depression and went around gathering buffalo chips, and dried bison droppings and tossing them back into the wallow. In the place of firewood, buffalo chips worked fine, and he had used them many times in the past.

Colt respected all the Indian nations, because they lived in harmony with nature. Every nation of warriors practiced self-controlled conservation methods. In earlier times, some tribes had made piles of stones and arranged them in a funnel, then chased a herd of buffalo into the funnel and run them over the cliff. That was wasteful but was about the only way they could harvest their meat then. After more sophisticated bows and other weapons were developed, they started taking individual animals. White men, on the other hand, were lining up on trains and shooting bison after bison from passing railroad cars. Such a demand developed for buffalo hides that hunters would kill thousands of buffalo, then take only the hides. Practices like this angered Chris, as the Indians knew they had to protect all herds of animals so there would always be a supply for their tribes.

As Colt lay in that buffalo wallow, trying to fall asleep, he remembered an incident that had occurred some years earlier.

Man Killer was a boy then and had been given the name Ezekiel by Christian missionaries who ministered to the Nez Percé. He and Colt had been pushing a herd of stolen Nez Percé Appaloosas to return them to Chief Joseph. They also were herding the rustlers who had stolen the horses.

Young Man Killer hesitated, and Colt yelled, "Go! Save the horses!"

Out of nowhere Chris felt an animal's presence nearby. It was close, but he couldn't pick up any sign of it.

Suddenly, with a tremendous roar and a rush,

a giant silvertip grizzly came out of the thicket on the uphill side of his trail. This monster stood over eight feel tall on its hindlegs and weighed well over a ton and a half.

A grizzly bear on level ground can outrun a racehorse for a short distance, and this big boar was no exception. He closed the distance between the thicket and his hiding place in seconds, and Colt barely had time to spin and fire from the hip. His bullet took the bruin in the front of the left shoulder with little or no effect.

The bear slammed against the rib cage of War Bonnet, his teeth popping and a roar emanating from deep in his chest that reverberated through the canyon. Colt flew sideways, and the horse rolled once and bolted toward the herd, scattering the ones in front of him. The boar stopped and stood on its hindlegs, nose testing the wind, while he swung his watermelon-sized head from side to side.

As the bear dropped to all fours, Chris raised his pistol, aiming at the bear's face. The bruin charged, Chris fired, yet the bullet glanced off the bear's skull, creating a crease along its head. It was as if it had been whacked with a fly swatter.

The bear slammed into Colt. Ironically, only the pistol saved Chris from the mighty teeth and jaws, as the bear bit down on the gun, mangling it.

Giving up the gun, Colt leaped away. He pulled his horn-handled bowie knife from the beaded sheath on his left hip and switched it to his right hand, facing the shaggy killer. The bear stared at Colt through his little pig eyes, while heavy breaths poured out between spike-sized teeth.

Colt felt no fear. Yes, the bear weighed hundreds and hundreds of pounds more than Colt and stood almost two feet taller. The scout, however, was a true warrior, and though he was staring death in the face, he was conditioned not to feel fear until the combat was over. His head was clear. His nerves were steady. Adrenaline coursed through his body, and he was prepared to match his wits and strength against this superior foe.

With a roar the bear charged. Colt stood his ground, and the big furry body slammed into Chris with tremendous force. As Colt was falling he struck upward with full power and jammed the big bowie into the bear's chest just behind the left front leg.

With agility that seemed incredible for its size, the grizzly jumped in the air with a loud roar and twisted its body at the same time, biting at the knife, which was buried to the hilt behind the joint. He rolled beyond Chris Colt, who lay unconscious on the ground, his head having slammed into a flat rock when the bear crashed into him.

At that, Chris stirred and sat up. He looked up at the sky over Kansas, seeing nothing but stars from horizon to horizon. Funny that he'd remember that bear . . .

Suddenly a chill ran down his spine. Chris Colt had a special feeling when being hunted. Animals also possessed this same feeling when they were prey for some predator. The only way Colt could ever describe the feeling to people was to remind them of some time in their life when they felt someone was staring at them and they would turn around and see someone there. Colt believed that this "sense of knowing" was a sixth sense, undeveloped in most people. Yet people who lived life on the edge developed the sense out of necessity. This was not a feeling of being watched. Rather, he felt that he was being hunted.

Out on the plains, a grizzly had become interested in the scent trail he now followed. It was man scent, but it also smelled of blood. He had picked up the scent in the little treed area where Colt had camped. The scent got stronger as the big bear followed the trail westward toward a distant buffalo wallow.

The bear had put on plenty of miles the previous day and evening. Those bears that roamed out on the plains had to travel a lot farther each day in search of food than those in the high country. He decided to nap after daylight in a buffalo wallow himself. The bear was storing fat for the winter and was not starving. On top of that, the trail he was following from the creek was man-smell, and that was not normal prey. His previous experiences with creatures with man-smell had been unpleasant. One time he had fed on a half-rotting carcass of an Arapaho warrior who had been out hunting and had fallen on one of his own arrows and bled to death. The bear, like other bears who had tried it, did not like the taste of human flesh, so it was easier for him to bed down and pursue the blood scent trail later.

Two miles away, Chris Colt pulled himself out of the buffalo wallow. With spear, pack, and water bags lashed across his back, Colt started hobbling westward, his eyes set on the far horizon. With elbows, forearms, and shoulders so sore that he winced with every movement, he kept on. He had been in tough circumstances before, and he knew how to get where he was going. He looked ahead for a distant clump or rock or bush and told himself he just had to make it that far. Once he reached that goal, he would pick out something else and go for that. He simply did this all day long and actually made pretty good time. Although he had been weak from the wounds, he was also quickly building up the particular muscles needed for crawling in the long time he had been taking to heal while in the grove of trees. Chris dragged himself along, thinking about his wife and children and all the good times. The more he saw Shirley in his mind, the faster he crawled. He was averaging between two and three miles per hour and man walking would walk three miles per hour, so Colt was proving that he was deserving of the legendary repute.

He also had proven many times that God had kept his eyes on him from time to time. This was one of those times. It was well into the afternoon when the grizzly awakened and continued on the blood trail. Another hour passed before he made it to the buffalo wallow. He circled it warily, moving out and away and then close in, and finally satisfied himself that he could walk up to the edge of the depression and see if his prey was in the bottom. The bear kept testing the wind and the heavy scent and went down into the wallow, sniffing every square inch. Although it was man scent, it was so powerful now he got excited and took off to the west. The bear's nose was so sensitive and the trail so fresh that he didn't even have to sniff the ground to smell out the trail.

Grizzly bears and black bears often travel as much as fifty miles per day, searching for food or males searching for females in estrus. The grizzly was trotting after an hour, the scent of the man getting fresher and fresher.

Chris Colt saw the encroaching sunset ahead. He was worn out. He had been hobbling all day long, and now he just wanted to lie down. He would eat some jerky and a wild turnip out of his pack and then sleep.

Out of longtime habit, Colt looked at his back trail. He gulped as he saw a large brown spot in the distance lumbering along his trail. He did not have to look any longer to know, even at that distance, that it was a grizzly.

Colt knew he had a spear, but he also felt he could only be blessed and protected in critical situations so many times. He simply was no match for a large grizzly.

Colt had talked to a few old-timers who told him that you could sometimes survive a grizzly attack if you rolled on your stomach and wrapped your arms around the back of your neck and simply play dead. They said that you would get chewed on and swatted around a little, but the grizzly would eventually lose interest and leave. Colt decided that this was his only option.

Then he thought about setting the prairie grass on fire, but he discarded the thought immediately. The prairie grass might burn for miles and burn out farmers and ranchers as well. He would not be that selfish.

Colt watched the beast approach, and he wondered if he could just play dead and not fight back. It was so against his nature, it would be very hard for him to do. Chris's heart stopped as he saw the big bear pause and stand on his hindlegs. At that distance, which was now a couple hundred yards, he knew the bear could not see him because they had such poor eyesight. Then he realized that the wind had just shifted. What was the boar smelling?

The bear had caught a whiff on the breeze that caught his attention. Only one thing could take a large boar grizzly's mind off food. She was about seven miles to the north, and the changing wind had brought her smell to the big boar. He forgot about the hot blood trail and took off on the wind searching out the sow grizzly in estrus.

Chris Colt saw him trotting north and figured out what was the cause. Once again he looked skyward and started praying gratefully. Now that the danger was past, he felt nauseated and his knees started shaking.

Chris wished for a cigarillo and a cup of coffee, then he rolled over on his back as the bear trotted out of sight.

He said aloud, "The hell with coffee and tobacco, Chris. You need about twenty shots of whiskey right now."

Colt decided that the bear either smelled stronger food with the wind shifting from the north, or he smelled a female, which was the most likely answer in his mind. Either way, though, he would soon return. Colt would take advantage of the opportunity and put as much distance between himself and the bear as possible.

Chris's adrenaline was pumping now, and he ignored the severe pain in his leg. His back was killing him, too. He moved westward as fast as he could. He was thankful to see that a full moon was going to be out and the sky was cloudless. It wouldn't have mattered if the night was pitch black to the grizzly, because his nose was his pair of eyes. Yet Chris was thankful that he could at least see his death coming ahead of time, and he found himself frequently looking back over his shoulders.

The hours passed, and Colt got so he felt like he could not drag himself another foot, but he kept on. Finally, he sank to the ground, and looked up at the sky. His breaths came out in pants as his chest heaved up and down, feeling like it was going to explode. Colt prayed again, asking for help. No sooner had he done that than he rolled over and saw something dark far ahead to the west. Colt moved his head down as close to the ground as possible. He looked along the ground with growing excitement. Ahead, in the distance, was a tree line.

The big bear was angry. He had found the sow, and she was in estrus, but she had another suitor, and that boar was even bigger. The big boar was not used to running into a bear bigger and tougher than himself. He tried to stand and fight, but the other boar eventually ran him off. Now the bear was headed due south and was not far from the blood scent trail he had found earlier. He didn't remember it; instinctively something made him head in that direction.

The big bruin came across an old rotting wagon, a common sight out on this empty prairie. The bear started smacking the wagon with his forepaws and sent splintered wood flying everywhere. He grabbed part of a wagon wheel and bit down on it, ignoring several splinters that went into his pink-and-black gums. The brute continued smacking the wagon and destroying it. He swept pieces of broken wagon along with clouds of dust with mighty sweeps of the dish-sized paws and, satisfied at last, headed south again.

Colt was making the tree line when the big bear got a whiff of man blood scent. It stood on its hindlegs and dropped down, huffing and popping his teeth. He started off after the quarry.

Chris Colt had that sense again that he was being followed and, turning, spotted the dark spot again in the distance. Chris started scrambling forward again, but now the tree crowns were rising up against the night sky ahead of him, giving him renewed hope.

The scent of man and beef and blood and the animal hides was so strong now, it excited the beast. He was angry at the man-smell, having transformed the earlier confrontation with the other boar, though he no longer had any memory of the incident.

The monster boar slowed slightly, preparing

to start circling his prey. He would test the wind from every direction to ensure that there were no hidden enemies, no surprises. When everything seemed right, then he'd close in.

Chris Colt knew this, and he watched as the bear circled off to the right, standing on his hindlegs before entering the tree line. Chris would make his final move into the trees while the bear was circling. Colt knew that his movement would be detected by the bear and would invite instant attack. That, too, was instinctive with bears and other large predators. The fleeing movement of a prey would trigger an instant attack response. Chris knew that he would have to use up the last of his energy to get up into a tree. Grizzly bears, except for their cubs, did not climb trees, and that was Colt's only chance.

The bear was out of sight in the blackness of the cottonwoods when Colt made his move. He heard the bear to the west of him now moving south. The bear stopped and stood up, testing the wind again. Colt stopped. Bears had poor eyesight and okay hearing, but he would soon be downwind of Colt and the strength of his scent might just bring the bear right in. The bear started moving again, and Colt moved to another tree, hoping to find some branches low enough to pull himself up. There were none.

Colt fought panic as he hobbled from tree to tree, knowing the bear had to be close. His mind worked quickly, trying to solve this emergency.

Chris then saw a sapling near a large tree. If he could climb the sapling and swing over to the cottonwood, maybe he could reach a branch. Colt grabbed the lower branches of the sapling and started pulling himself up. Up he went, hand over hand, even though he was convinced that his arms were so worn out, he thought he could not make it.

Colt had climbed as high as he could when he suddenly felt a sharp tug on his right foot. He looked down. The grizzily was directly below him, both paws on the sapling and Colt's moccasin in his teeth. Chris's eyes opened as wide as a .45-70 hole through a tin of peaches. He started swinging the sapling, back and forth, but could not quite make it over to the other tree. Meanwhile, the big bear shook the tree and swatted at it, the force of his blows almost jarring Colt's grip loose.

Colt's mind was calm and clear as he searched for another solution. He suddenly had one. Holding on for dear life, he reached up behind his back and started untying the spear he carried. He finally got it loose, and at the same time, he noticed that the growling bear below was chewing angrily on the sapling trunk. The big bruin's teeth were doing more damage, more quickly, than a lumberjack with a new ax. Chris realized that the sapling would soon fall, and he had to make it on the first try. Chris got the spear untied finally. He grabbed it in his right hand, and as the sapling rocked forward, he threw it as hard as he could at the cottonwood. The spear struck through the bark. He swayed back, hearing a cracking down below. He went forward with another cracking sound, and his hand shot out, grabbing the end of the spear. He pulled hard and the spear held. As the sapling bent forward toward the bigger tree, Chris saw a branch slightly above him. To reach it, though, he would have to let go of the sapling and risk falling to certain death. He didn't even hesitate. Colt yanked hard with his arms, and he grabbed the branch and pulled himself across. Just then the grizzly pulled the sapling down with a loud cracking sound and he started thrashing the tree and biting it everywhere.

Chris leaned down from the branch and grabbed the spear in his left hand and started prying it out. The bear now gave his attention to Colt in his almost-reachable perch. The grizzly reached as high as he could and tried desperately to dig in his claws and pull himself up-

ward, but it could not be done. Chris Colt held
the spear high overhead and waited. The bear
let out a mighty roar of frustration and rage,
and Colt thrust downward. The spear went right
into the open mouth, partway down the esophagus, and pierced the upper lobes of the right
lung. Colt, still holding the end of the spear,
yanked it back up out the bear's throat. The animal, whose roar was choked off by the thrust,
dropped down on all fours and swatted the tree
like a boxer on hands and knees. Chris threw
the spear down, but it glanced off the side of
the animal. The grizzly turned its head with a
roar and bit at the bloody gash. The bear disappeared into the darkness of the trees. Colt listened to him thrashing around for a long time.

Colt tried to make himself comfortable on the
big branch and found a small branch above,
which he was able to hang his pack on. He
drank up the rest of his water from the second
bladder and waited. The lawman knew that he
could not fall asleep for fear of falling from his
perch. There was no way he would try to crawl
down either until broad daylight. The last thing
he wanted to do was try to determine in the
darkness if a wounded thousand-pound killing
machine was dead or not.

Colt prayed that the bear was dead, because

he was freezing now with the cold front that had moved in. If the bear was indeed dying, Colt relished the thought of a bear skin coat, moccasins, meat, and he even decided he would make himself a bear claw necklace like the Lakotah he had lived with.

Chris sat on the branch and thought about his wife and children all night long. After sunup, Colt decided to wait until full daylight before trying to go down. He had not heard the bear for hours. Would the big bear be laying in wait? Grizzlies often did that.

An hour later, Colt decided he should go down the tree, but he had not planned on a descent. It was too far down and there were no branches to let him easily descend. Chris finally climbed down to the branch below him on the other side of the tree and started easing himself down the branch. He was wearing his pack on his back. Colt was nervous, but this branch was long enough that he felt it could let him down almost to the ground if he crawled out far enough. He inched forward and the branch slowly started dipping down toward the ground. Chris was further relieved to see that there were some thick bushes below the end of the branch, so if he had to drop, it might be onto the bushes. The branch sank lower and lower. Colt finally grabbed the branch in both hands and swung down through the twigs and leaves and dropped another couple of feet, twisting his body so he landed on top of the bushes. He rolled and felt solid ground.

Christ hobbled to the spear immediately and pulled it out of the ground. It was the only chance he would have had for survival against the grizzly if the beast was laying in wait for him somewhere nearby. Colt had scoured the ground with his eyes while up in the tree and saw no sign of him, but the undergrowth was thick because there was a small stream running through the trees. The whole wooded area was only a few acres in size, and he could look through the trees from one side to the other and see more empty prairie.

Clutching the spear, Colt hobbled forward along the bear's trail. Colt was finally rewarded with a sight that made his heart leap. The cool breeze from the north whipped some brown hairs, with silvertips on the end, back and forth above some brush. It was the grizzly. Colt picked up a stick and threw it, hitting the bear's body. It did not move. Colt had no way of knowing that his spear had pierced the bruin's lung yet, if he had been able to follow him the night before, he would have seen the telltale

bright red blood with bubbles in it, indicating a
good lung hit. After so many hours, the blood
was all dry now and dark brown. He threw another stick, and the bear still did not move. It
looked like Colt was going to make it through
the winter.

CHAPTER 9

Going Home

Man Killer wrapped his Hudson's Bay blanket around him even tighter as the chilly wind struck at him, stinging his face with snow and cold. Hawk, his big black Appaloosa, high-stepped briskly through the drifting snow, which came up to his belly in some places. Man Killer held onto the lead line of his packhorse as they headed toward the distant tree line. He would have to make camp and have shelter until the storm passed. Chris Colt had been missing for several months now, and Man Killer had not found him, if he was still alive by some miracle, or found his body if the inevitable had occurred.

An hour later, Man Killer yanked his Winchester from the boot and placed it across the swell of his saddle as he approached the trees. He thought he had seen a tendril of smoke rising up through the branches. He approached carefully. He came upon a fire and a large lean-to. A man sat with his back to him, wearing a buffalo coat and a hat made from grizzly bear hide. He was drinking coffee, and Man Killer saw steam coming off an earthenware pot on the fire. A handmade bow and quiver of arrows leaned against the tree nearby, and there was a spear made of chipped stone.

Suddenly the man, without looking, spoke. To Man Killer, the words seemed to be coming from a deep-voiced angel. "Well, you going to inch up here or come in and have some chicory coffee? I've been waiting for months. You bring any tobacco and real coffee?"

Man Killer, who had never cursed in his life, yelled enthusiastically, "Hell, yes, Great Scout!"

He was glad that Colt's back was turned so he could quickly brush away the tears from his eyes.

Man Killer dismounted and immediately grabbed a large coffeepot and grounds from a packsaddle, along with a pouch and tobacco papers. He walked up and poured water into the pot and set it on the fire. As he held out the tobacco and papers to Colt, Man Killer was shocked. Colt had a very long beard. He also had lost weight and had dark circles under his eyes. Man Killer eyed the giant grizzly bear claws hanging from the fur in the necklace around Colt's neck. Yes, the scout had survived.

Colt made a cigarette and lit it, inhaling deeply. It made him light-headed, but he did not care. He enjoyed the taste and simple pleasure of the smoke. War Bonnet untied his lead line with his teeth and eagerly trotted over to his master, trying to lift Colt with his nose. Chris threw his arms around the big horse's neck and hugged him for several minutes.

Man Killer sat across from Colt on the log and made himself a cigarette, too. Both men smoked in peace, not speaking for some time.

Not until they both had a steaming cup of coffee in their hands did Man Killer finally say, "They all believe you are dead. I knew you had to be alive. I could not give up looking."

Colt's voice was husky and broke slightly when he said, "Hell, I know that."

Man Killer said, "I found an old camp and the skeletons of antelope in the camp many miles to the east. How long did it take you to walk here?"

Colt said, "I didn't walk. I crawled."

Man Killer had all his answers with that one statement. He understood everything that had gone on by what Colt had just said, and the bear claw necklace.

Man killer said, "Phineas Clarke and his gang are dead."

Colt said, "Good. Who sent them to Hell?"

Man Killer said, "We did. Joshua, Charlotte and I tracked them down in Trinidad. They had bragged that they killed you."

Chris said, "This is a good thing, my brother."

Man Killer said, "How many bullets were in you?"

Colt said, "Seventeen, but that was months ago. We need to think about today and tomorrow now."

Man Killer knew to change the subject but was once again amazed by his mentor.

Sheepishly, he asked, "Do you still crawl?"

Colt said, "No, my thighs were broken by two bullets, but one bullet worked its way out and festered until I dug it out with a sharp stick. Thank God for Indian poultices or I would have gone under after that one. I was out of it with infection for a few days there. The other bullet, I think, probably will always be stuck in my thigh bone but both legs are healed now and I can walk. Once the snow started coming, though, I knew I had to winter here. Thank God for a big old grizzly and a loner buffalo that both walked in here and died of heart attacks."

Man Killer laughed.

Colt stared off at the far horizon and summoned up the courage to ask, "Do my kids think I'm dead?"

Man Killer smiled, "Great Scout, nobody in your family believes you have died. All others believe it, but not your family, and not Tex Westchester. He has told everyone you were holed up for the winter and will show up in the springtime."

Chris smiled.

Man Killer went on, "Emily dropped a piece of wood on her foot before Christmas and broke two toes, but she is better now. All others in your family are fine."

Colt said, "Any more word on the rest of the gang?"

Man Killer said, "We can speak of this later. It is time to go home now and rest. You must get strong again."

Colt said, "Believe me, my friend, I am a lot stronger. I'm just worn out."

Man Killer walked to War Bonnet and started unloading the packs. He had used Chris Colt's saddle with the stirrups tied under the paint's

belly and lashed on the big panniers with dia-
mond hitches.

Colt got up to help, but Man Killer said,
"Please wait. I want to do this."

Man Killer reached into one of the big packs
and pulled out Colt's Peacemakers, holster, and
knives. He handed them to Chris, then brought
out his buckskins. Next, he pulled out a store-
house of food and Colt's Winchester. Chris's
eyes glistened as if he were an orphan given a
prince's Christmas party.

Man Killer then walked over to Colt and said,
"But first, this," as he handed Chris a large bar
of soap.

Colt chuckled and started stripping off his
clothes. Man Killer noticed that Colt's already
bulging arm muscles were even bigger, but what
was incredible were the bullet scars all over his
back, buttocks, and the back of his legs and
arms, as he walked toward the little pond he
had created by damming the creek. Man Killer
watched as Chris Colt used a rock and broke
through the thin layer of ice and plunged into
the water. Colt quickly bathed and rinsed, then
tiptoed briskly through the snow and stood
naked in front of the fire, feeding logs on top
of it.

From the packs Man Killer produced a pan

and put more water on to boil. He also produced a small mirror, which he hung from the
stub of a branch on a tree near the campfire.

After the water was hot, Colt pulled out his
bowie and asked, "Sharpen it?"

Man Killer gave him a look of mock insult.

Colt smiled and dipped the soap into the
water and lathered up his long beard. He started
shaving with the blade of the big knife. When
he finished, Man Killer handed him a flask of
whiskey, and the scout-turned-lawman splashed
it on his face, wincing with the sting.

The Nez Percé teased, "Mighty Scout, have
you never felt pain before?"

With that, Colt shot him a sidelong glance and
the two started laughing. It turned into hysteria,
with both of them falling beside the fire and
holding their sides.

Roaring with laughter, Colt ignored all the
scars crisscrossing and dotting his entire body
and pointed to his right index finger, saying,
"Yeah, look here. I got a splinter in that last
week, and it really hurt like the dickens."

The tears spilling down their cheeks were
from laughter, but they were also tears of relief
and of love between two close friends.

* * *

Word spread all over southern Colorado before Chris Colt and Man Killer arrived. Colt had first stopped at a hospital in Denver. He was given lots of liquids and plenty of steaks and potatoes. The doctor warned him that he would experience soreness and stiffness in many of his joints whenever there was a rain or snowstorm coming, and that maybe someday the remaining bullet in his leg might try to work its way out. All in all, however, Colt had fully recovered. The bullets in his back had missed vital organs, and his spine was untouched. The doctors felt that he would continue to walk and ride normally and the splint had really helped his leg heal straight. Colt was released to go home after a few days' rest and strict warnings about building his strength back up.

When Chris Colt and Man Killer rode up the driveway to the Colt ranch, Chris was surprised to see his children, Charley and her girls, Joshua, Tex, Jennifer, his attorney Brandon Rudd and his wife, Elizabeth, along with several others from Canon City, Silver Cliff, and Westcliffe.

The greeting party stood by the big house, smiling at the man who was returning from the dead.

Joseph and Brenna could not contain themselves any further. They dashed forward with Brenna screaming, "Daddy! Daddy!"

He jumped down off War Bonnet and swept both of them up in his arms. He hugged them tightly, kissing them both over and over. It embarrassed Joseph, but he did not care just then. Colt then remounted and reached down to his children. He pulled Joseph up behind him, and Brenna sat in front of him. They rode up to the house amidst the cheers and tears of his family and friends. Charlotte ran up and threw herself into her big brother's arms and cried on his massive chest, while he held and comforted her. Her little girls came up and hugged his legs, and he lifted each one and gave them a hug. Then he hugged the rest of the women and shook hands with the men. Joshua was last. He walked up to his brother, and the two gave each other grins that spoke volumes. They grabbed each other's shoulders and clasped hands, both smiling broadly.

Quietly, Joshua said, "Welcome home, brother."

Chris said, "Thanks. Thanks for everything."

Charlotte walked over and said, "What now?"

Chris said, "I have two more to get, Buck Fuller and Aramus Randall. Aramus was the one who killed Shirley. He was the leader."

Charlotte said, "They're both in Montana."

Chris replied, "Man Killer told me. I'm going to build myself back up a little, then I'll leave."

Charley said, "I'm going with you this time, Chris."

Colt sharply said, "No," then more calmly, added, "No, I have this to do alone."

The next morning, before breakfast, the lawman was outside, bare-chested with light snowflakes slowly falling down. He was splitting firewood and was sweating to boot. Tex and Joshua both tried to offer him help as they walked by for breakfast, but Colt declined. He wanted to get built back up, and the firewood was a small part of it. That was for his upper body. Chris wanted to build his legs back up, and that would begin about an hour after breakfast when Colt started running toward the looming range.

Chris spent a while after breakfast with Joshua and Charley getting caught up on all the happenings during all the months he had been gone. After that, Colt went outside and whistled for Kuli, his big pet timberwolf. Within minutes the large canine appeared with blood on the hairs around his mouth and nose. Colt knew it was not from any livestock or the barn cats, because Kuli was shown that all of them were part of his pack, just like the family was.

Kuli wagged his tail excitedly while Chris fussed over and petted him and scratched his ears.

Colt said, "Want to go for a run, boy?"

The wolf wagged its tail harder than ever. Colt left his six-shooters and strapped on his Cheyenne bow and quiver of arrows. With all the animals, such as grizzlies, in the Sangre de Cristos, he did not want to run up into them unarmed, but on the other hand, he did not want to be burdened down with heavy guns while running. He also had his bowie strapped diagonally in a sheath between his shoulder blades.

Chris started walking fast, heading slightly uphill toward the range just west of his home. The pastures of the Coyote Run gave way to massive stands of scrub oak, which gave way to evergreens on the base of the slopes. The ground at the ranch house was close to eight thousand feet in elevation, but only five miles away the elevation rose to over fourteen thousand feet. Every morning and evening hundreds of mule deer came out of the scrub oak thickets and dark timber areas to graze on the Colt lush green meadowland, alongside the herds of hundreds of brood mares that were bred to the top-line quarter-horse stallions of the colts and the Appaloosa stallions of Man Killer. Right then very few were grazing because it was close to spring and that was the snowiest time of the year in southern Colorado. Grasses didn't really start coming up until close to May.

After five minutes, Colt switched from walking to the slow jog he had learned from the Apaches. Running gradually uphill, Colt felt pretty good, except for the front of his thighs and bottom of his calf muscles. After a half hour, he really started sucking wind, but he refused to give up. He set a goal to keep going, no matter how much it hurt, until he reached a small beaver lake he knew of in a large stand of aspens. He spotted a tree with a heart and his initials and Shirley's carved in it. Tears spilled down his cheeks.

After Colt made it, he and Kuli lay side by side on the shore of the pond, sides heaving and lungs aching for oxygen. After catching their breath, Colt petted the big wolf for a while and watched a pair of beavers working together, but that made him think of his wife. Abruptly he jumped to his feet.

He said, "Come on, boy. Going downhill will be a lot easier."

The big canine ran alongside again as the sore and tired lawman headed back toward the ranch.

Chris Colt kept up the running every day, as well as repairing fences and splitting firewood. By the last snowfall of the spring, he had regained all the strength in his legs. He was running almost to timberline and back each day. During this time he took War Bonnet out of his comfortable stall and put him out in one of the big pastures where he could run and play and exercise with some of the stallions and geldings. Then, when Colt knew he was ready, he started taking War Bonnet up into the mountains for a morning run instead of running himself. This toned the big horse for the trying days ahead.

One morning Colt told Joseph and Brenna that he would ride with them to school. Brenna now had her own horse, a beautiful golden palomino named Sunshine. Chris and Shirley had originally intended to give Joseph a pony, when Man Killer gave the boy the Appaloosa gelding. Man Killer, very learned in horse rearing from his nation, the Nez Percé, explained that ponies are more often mean-spirited than horses. He told them that Joseph, and Brenna when she was old enough, would be much better off with a horse that they could get attached to and still ride as they got older. He also suggested that the Colts first make each child ride bareback for a year until they developed good leg aids, balance, and a rhythm with the horse. After that, he recommended tying the stirrups underneath the horse's brisket for another month or two until the child learned how to develop balance and rhythm with the horse while in the saddle. By doing this, the rider would learn how to properly squeeze the horse's ribs with their legs, and how to use the legs to control and ride without becoming dependent on the stirrups.

Brenna was now going through the bareback phase on Sunny, and Joseph was an outstanding rider with a fancy saddle that many cowboys would give their eyeteeth for. It had been reworked by a silversmith who had replaced the silver studs that Joseph had pried off and used to leave a trail marked for his father.

As they rode along, Chris Colt tried to explain what he was about to do. He was amazed when his little boy suddenly said, "Pa, when are you leaving, tomorrow morning?"

Chris smiled and shook his head, "Yes, son, there are two members left, and one of them was the one who stabbed your mother."

Joseph said, "Good, Pa, you need to find them and kill them both."

Chris was startled and looked straight ahead as they continued riding on. He kneed War Bonnet into a canter and said, "Come on, we better get to the school before classes start."

They rode hard beside their father and arrived at the schoolyard shortly thereafter. Chris shook hands with Joseph, then pulled him to him for a hug, then gave Brenna a hug and kiss. He headed to the mercantile in Silver Cliff to do some business, then let War Bonnet stretch his legs on a nice run back to the ranch.

Joseph sent Brenna into the school and asked the school marm if he could speak to her privately. Explaining that he would return shortly, he said that he had to run an emergency errand. She allowed it and he resaddled his horse and took off through Westcliffe and headed south toward the ranch of Man Killer and Jennifer Banta.

Running up to the training corral where Man Killer was lounging a beautiful red roan Appaloosa mare, Joseph slid Spot to a stop next to the round training ring.

Man Killer said, "Hello, Little Colt, how are you today?"

Joseph said, "I'm fine, Man Killer. I have to hurry; I gave my word."

Man Killer smiled and thought to himself, this is the son of Chris Colt.

Joseph said, "I came to tell you like you asked, Pa is leaving tomorrow morning."

Man Killer smiled and said, "Thank you, my little brother. I will see you at daybreak tomorrow."

Joseph grinned, then he tossed Chris Colt's U.S. marshal badge to Man Killer. The Indian nodded, grinning broadly.

He said, "You have done well."

Joseph waved as he turned his horse and dashed out of the driveway.

CHAPTER 10

Aramus

Chris Colt kissed Brenna on the forehead and tiptoed down the hallway. He was heading toward the back door, picking up his sack of food on the way, when he was stopped at the door by the sight of his little boy standing before him. Joseph walked forward and hugged his father.

Stepping back, Joseph said, "Careful, Pa. Brenna and me need you back here."

Chris tousled Joseph's hair, saying, "Don't you worry, son. I will be back before you know it."

Walking outside, he headed for the main barn, where he had already saddled War Bonnet and a packhorse. Colt was surprised to see Man Killer walk out of the barn leading the horses.

Chris said, "Man Killer, I appreciate it, partner, but this job is for me to do alone."

Man Killer reached in his shirt pocket and produced Colt's federal badge and tossed it to him. Then he rode up and handed over the reins to War Bonnet. Chris swung up into the saddle.

Man Killer looked at the badge and said, "No, that is your job, and I am your deputy. Let us go, Great Scout."

Chris said, "One of the two is the man who killed my wife, Man Killer. I don't want my badge right now."

Man Killer said, "You cannot tell your son to shoot only bucks so there will always be many deer, then shoot every fawn and doe that you see."

Colt said, "Man Killer, thanks, but I—"

Man Killer interrupted, "I see. You believe in the law of the white man, except for your family. So tell me old friend, why should I then live by the white man's law if you do not?"

Colt was getting exasperated. "Because your society would not exist if they don't live by the white man's law."

Man Killer said, "In my society, we would hunt down and kill the men who murdered your wife. What does your law say about that?"

Colt said, "Our law says that you cannot. They must be arrested and tried. But this is different."

"Yes, it is, Great Scout. You are what is called a lawman. You are supposed to represent the law. You are supposed to believe that the western frontier, as the white man calls it, will become better for men, red and white, to live in if men learn to respect the law. This is what you have taught me. Except, if you have not been treated right by bad things in life, you can change the law to make you feel better. You can forget your children and not allow those around you to help, because you must do this alone. So you go after these men to kill each one, and your children, who have already lost their mother, cry every day you are gone because they do not want to lose their father, too. You get wounded many times, and every person tells your children you have died, but they try bravely not to believe that, but you never come home, because you have to do this alone. And if you do not die, your children also worry that you will be arrested and go to jail and hang, because the law is not what you believe in anymore."

Chris Colt set his jaw and clenched his teeth. He roared, "All right, damn you! Get down off that horse!"

Man Killer jumped out of the saddle and stood in front of Colt, a small smile on his dark handsome face. He said, "Now, I have made you angry, so you will kill me, too? Is this another new law you have made for yourself?"

Chris started toward Man Killer, both fists clenched, and the young warrior stood his ground, but inside he was more scared than he had ever been in his life. Before Colt could even swing, though, the full weight of Man Killer's words hit him.

Chris Colt broke down and started crying. He was embarrassed doing this in front of Man Killer, but he could not help himself. He said, sobbing, "But she was my wife. I loved that woman so much."

Man Killer said, "So did I. But since I was a boy I have looked at you like my father. I have seen you always stand up for your law, and you have made me believe that your law can work, if men are brave enough to make it work. You would fight a great bear with your hands to save your child or another. You would have a gunfight with ten men on a principle and you would not run. But now you must ask yourself, Great Scout, are you brave enough to do what you believe in?"

Colt said, "That's a good question."

Man Killer went on. "If you can be brave and stand by your belief in the law of the white man, when your life has been thrown into the cooking fire, then are you not truly a man?"

Colt sat there on the grass in his backyard and lit up a cigarillo. He handed one to Man Killer, who sat down by him. They both smoked and looked up at the big range.

Colt said, "You are my friend, another brother. I am sorry I almost attacked you."

Man Killer replied, "You know my people do not apologize. It is understood without speaking of it. I knew you were not angry with me, but another."

Chris said, "Who?"

Man Killer said, "Chris Colt."

Colt laughed and said, "We better pack some more grub for you."

Man Killer said, "I have. Are you ready to go?"

Colt said, "I thank you for your words. Somehow you inherited the wisdom of Young Chief Joseph."

They mounted up and started down the driveway. Brenna opened her eyes and saw her brother kneeling with his head peeking out of the second-floor bedroom window.

Brenna said, "What are you doing, Joseph?"

He said, "Watching Man Killer be a good

friend. You know how Pa is the smartest man in the world when he stops and thinks real hard?"

Brenna said, "Yes?"

Joseph said, "I just saw Pa think real hard."

Colt and Man Killer turned right and headed south toward Westcliffe. They would ride to Canon City, and take the train there the next morning. First they rode to Pueblo and then switched trains to one heading north to Wyoming. They had been told, several times, that Aramus Randall and Buck Fuller had both been seen in the Jackson Hole area.

Many times when traveling long distances by train, Colt and Man Killer simply boarded a boxcar or livestock car with their horses, but this time they rode in a passenger car while the horses rode in the back. The train had stops in Colorado City, Castle Rock, Denver, and Fort Collins before passing into Wyoming. The two lawmen offloaded at Cheyenne, where the eastern plains of Colorado gave way to gently rolling grasslands.

Instead of heading up through Casper and cutting over to the Jackson Hole country, Colt decided they should ride straight cross-country through Laramie and cross the North Platte River at Rawlins, a trip of several days. They'd camp under the stars, and their meals would be cooked over a fire. Colt did not want the word getting ahead that he and Man Killer were headed toward Jackson Hole.

It was cold near the shining Grand Teton Mountain range, which to Colt were the most beautiful peaks after those in the Sangre de Cristos. At the base of the Grand Tetons, which seemed to be steeper overall and more jagged than most of the Sangres, Colt and Man Killer rode through tall evergreen and hardwood timber, real elk country. The timberline was lower in the Grand Tetons, because they were farther north. For that reason they seemed as tall as the Sangre de Cristos, which in fact contained some of the tallest peaks in the Rockies.

After Man Killer's talk with him, Chris Colt did a lot of thinking. When he had been riding with his children to school the day before he and Man Killer left, it had really bothered him a lot when his little boy told him he needed to kill the two men. What was he teaching his children? he wondered.

Once outside Jackson, they decided Man Killer would go into town by himself, knowing that Colt would be recognized. In addition, the Nez Percé rode on their packhorses, so nobody would notice his big Appaloosa, Hawk, and figure out who he was. He nosed around town for several hours until he finally struck up a conversation with an old Crow, who worked odd jobs around town.

The old man sat on a bale of bedding straw in the livery stable while he worked on a trace harness for a freighter. Man Killer rolled him a smoke and handed it to him, already lit. He made himself a cigarette, too.

The old man said, "Good tobacco."

Man Killer blew a puff skyward and nodded affirmatively.

The old man said, "White man is stupid."

Man Killer said, "Why do you say that?"

"Because it is true."

Man Killer chuckled and said, "Oh."

Then the old Crow repeated, "White man is stupid."

Man Killer didn't reply, so the Crow said again, "Good tobacco, but with much money like you, man can buy good tobacco."

Man Killer looked askance and said, "What do you mean?"

The old man said, "What I said."

"But why did you say 'much money'?"

"See leaves on trees yonder?"

Man Killer looked at several trees growing near the stable and nodded.

The old man said, "The leaves are like your dollars in the bank."

Man Killer finally said, "Do you know me?"

"Now I do," the Crow said. "We have just spoken. I am Long-Legged Bear."

Man Killer said, "My name is—"

The old man interrupted, "Man Killer of Chief Joseph's tribe of the Nez Percé."

Man Killer said, "How do you know me?"

Long-Legged Bear said, "It is my job."

"What is your job?"

"To know things."

"Why?"

Long-Legged Bear said, 'Why do you think I live in this town, because I like the white man?"

Man Killer laughed. "To learn things, I guess."

The old man said, "I like this tobacco. It is good."

Man Killer made himself another cigarette, then gave the rest of his tobacco and papers to the old warrior.

The Crow said, "What is it you seek?"

"I did not say I seek anything."

"Yes, you did."

Man Killer shook his head, saying, "No, I did not."

Long-Legged Bear said, "Yes, you did, young man."

"What did I say?"

"You said you want me to tell you something."

Man Killer said, "You've been drinking fire-water, old man."

"That would be a good thing," the Crow said, chuckling. Then he added, "You did not speak with your mouth."

Man Killer started to wonder if this man was Chief Joseph's bastard brother on liquor. "How did I ask you to tell me something without using my mouth?"

The old man said, "Do the Nez Percé and the Crow build our lodges together? Do our peoples make great circles on banks of mighty rivers? Do the Pierced Noses and the Crow share our cooking fires and great hunts together?"

Man Killer said, "No."

Long-Legged Bear said, "Did I bring you a good war pony and a stout bow when you married the white woman with the hair from the sun?"

Man Killer grinned and said, "No, I just met you."

Long-Legged Bear then said, "Why did you give me the good tobacco of Man Killer?"

Man Killer started to answer quickly, but caught himself. He stopped and laughed at himself. "Because I wanted to ask you questions."

The old man took a long puff on his cigarette. Blowing a blue stream of smoke skyward, he studied it carefully, and finally spoke. "Do you worry that I will tell the white men here who you are? Where does your brother the great Colt wait for you, out in the trees yonder? Perhaps by the river? He speaks to the fish and says my name is Colt and they will jump out of the river, so he will not come after them."

Man Killer said, "Should I worry?"

The Crow said, "Why ask?"

"I'd like to know."

"You know already."

Man Killer thought for a moment and said, "You will help me because I am red also."

"See," the old man said, "you already knew. What do you wish?"

Man Killer said, "Chris Colt is white."

The old warrior made another cigarette while Man Killer patiently waited, and made a ceremony of lighting it. He took two deep puffs before he finally answered.

"No, he is not white."

"Of course he is."

The old man said, "No, he is not white, just

his skin is. His heart is red like yours and mine."

Man Killer thought about this simple, profound statement and smiled. The old man was right. "We are looking for two men. Their skin is brown. One is named Aramus Randall and the other is Buck Fuller."

Long-Legged Bear said, "They are men who live still who killed the woman of Colt."

Man Killer nodded solemnly.

"The younger man is simple in his mind, I think." Man Killer listened intently as the old man went on. "The older one is a man with no honor, but he has the heart of great bear. He will fight hard."

Man Killer said, "Then he will die."

Long-Legged Bear said, "This one will die."

Man Killer knew now that the man was going to help him, so he waited patiently for answers to come. This was the Indian way.

"Tell me, if you were the killer of the woman of Colt, where would you go around here?"

Man Killer said, "Into the mountains."

"And how would you hide from Colt?"

"You cannot."

"You know that," he said, "but do men who are stupid and kill the woman of Colt, do they know?"

"No, I guess they are stupid enough to think they would be smarter than Colt."

"So," Long-Legged Bear asked, "if you were the stupid men, where do you think you would go in the mountains to hide and make money?"

Man Killer thought, then asked, "Trapping?"

The old man said, "If you were stupid, would you be smart enough to know that Colt would indeed find you trapping?"

Man Killer said, "Yes."

"So where in the mountains would you hide?"

The Nez Percé said, "I don't know. In the trees?"

The old man came back, "Would Colt find you in the trees?"

"Yes."

"Then," Long-Legged Bear continued, "where in the mountains could you make money but Colt could not find you?"

Man Killer didn't see what the old Crow was getting at. Long-Legged Bear sensed this.

"If you were a man who was stupid and killed the wife of the mighty Colt, you might think you could hide in the mountain."

"But where in the mountain?" Man Killer pleaded.

"In the mountain."

Man Killer finally caught on, saying, "In the mountain. Working in a mine?"

The old man blew another stream of smoke out and grinned, nodding. "Would not such a man think that he could hide inside the mountain?"

Man Killer said, "Do you know the name of the mine they are working at?"

Long-Legged Bear said, "I did not speak of they."

Man Killer said, "Then where is Buck Fuller?"

The old man again hesitated, then said, "If you were the chief of these men. If you knew Colt was coming after you. If you were hiding in the mountain, would you be able to see Colt if he came up?"

"No," Man Killer replied, "you can't. You're underground."

Long-Legged Bear said, "Then how could you have eyes that would see Colt while you are inside the mountain?"

Man Killer said, "His partner, Buck."

The old man said, "Where would you have him stay so he could see Colt and warn you, and he could make money?"

Man Killer said, "I would figure Colt would be coming the way we came. I would have him stay right here maybe. Yes, right here in Jackson.

Then he could ride out to give a warning when Colt was spotted."

The old man puffed thoughtfully on his cigarette and blew the smoke skyward.

Then Man Killer said, "Where does he stay? Does he work in this town?"

Long-Legged Bear said, "If you were simple in your mind and you had skin that is brown and you lived here, where would you find work?"

Man Killer said, "Let me see. Probably only shoveling manure or, wait, does he work here in this livery stable?"

"Maybe," the old Crow warrior said, "he rides with the owner of this livery to bring wagons of alfalfa and maybe come back tomorrow, maybe the day after."

Man Killer was excited. He pulled out a gold double-eagle and placed it in Long-Legged Bear's palm, saying, "When you run out of tobacco, buy more."

Long-Legged Bear said, "You see, young man. I was not needed. You already had all the answers in your head."

Man Killer laughed, swung up, and took off for the camp by the river.

As he approached the camp, it was dark in the trees, but he saw the glow of the fire flickering and dancing on leaves overhead. This bothered him very much, because Colt lived by the credo, "White man builds big fire and stands back. He burns his face and freezes his back, but the wise Indian builds small fire and stays warm all over."

Man Killer rode up to where Hawk and War Bonnet stood in the trees. He dismounted. Walking forward, he yelled, "Do not shoot! This is a friendly redskin!"

At first there was no response, and Man Killer stopped, drawing a gun.

Then Colt yelled out, "Come on in, Uncha! I was just sleeping near the fire!"

Man Killer started backing up slowly and yelled out, "I will be right there. I must unsaddle and put that medicine on the horse's behind!"

Colt's Lakotah name was Wamble Uncha, or One Eagle, and Uncha meant "One," so Man Killer knew that Colt was saying that there was only one and he was "near the fire."

With his words Man Killer had told Colt that he would sneak in and come up behind them.

He grabbed his Winchester from the saddle boot and took off at a stiff-legged trot, running on the balls of his feet. He circled around the camp, cocking his carbine while he was out of earshot. He raced forward, watching the fire-light, and slowed down greatly as he got closer.

Near the fire Man Killer saw a short, stocky man with a red beard holding a Smith & Wesson .44 on Colt, who had his hands raised. Man Killer kept creeping closer and closer, until he was close enough to spit on the man.

The man whispered to Colt, "Where's thet damned red nigger? Holler out to 'im."

Colt said, "No."

The red-beard said, "What?"

Colt said, "No."

Red said, "You see this .44, boy?"

Colt said, "Yeah, I do, boy."

The man's face started getting as red as his beard. "You must have a death wish, lawman. Thet why ya don't wanna call that blanket nigger?"

Man Killer spoke up at last. "No, it is because the blanket nigger is behind you with a Winchester .44 pointed at your spine and is ready to blow a hole through your dirty white skin. Drop the gun."

The man shocked, but trying to keep his voice steady, said, "I'm aiming at your partner. You drop your gun and come in here in front of me with your hands grabbing clouds, and I'll let him live."

Man Killer said, "No."

Red said, "What do ya mean no?"

Man Killer said, "No. He is not my friend. He is just another white man. I do not care when you white men kill each other."

The thief said, "Then how come you went to the trouble a sneakin' up on me?"

Man Killer said, "Because he owes me money. I made a buffalo coat for him, and he has not paid me. So go ahead and shoot him, but I will still shoot you. Now, think quickly, because when I say the number five, I will shoot you dead. You can take the other white man to hell with you when you go, I don't care. One, two, three, four—"

"Wait!" the man yelled, dropping his gun as if it were a flaming ember he had picked out of the fire. He stuck his hands up in the air, and Man Killer walked forward.

Colt said, grinning, "You came right on time, partner."

Man Killer said, "But how did he get the drop on you, Great Scout?"

The bearded man said, "Great scout! You have to be kidding. I put the sneak on him while he had dropped his drawers and was takin' a dump back behind the bushes."

Man Killer burst out with laughter. He

pointed at Colt, who was retrieving his gun belt. Man Killer laughed so hard tears ran down his cheeks, and he continued to look over at Colt and point at him. Every time he did that, Colt would grind his teeth together so hard it almost broke them. His face was also as red as a tomato. This made Man Killer laugh even harder.

The holdup man made a move for his gun but stopped short when Colt drew his gun and cocked it. Still laughing, Man Killer got manacles from one of the packs and placed them on the man's wrists, looping the chain behind a tree near the fire.

Then he faced Colt, who had taken a seat on a log near the fire, and Man Killer said, "Let me understand, Great Scout, famous gunfighter, revered lawman, Christopher Colt, did that man sneak up on you and get the drop on you while you were going to the bathroom?"

Colt's face got even redder, and he really gritted his teeth together, saying, "It could have happened to you."

Man Killer laughed even more, as he said, "I don't think so."

The laughing finally subsided and they, under the cover of darkness, took the would-be robber into town, checked the livery stable, and returned to camp again. They also had a talk with the town marshal about not revealing their presence for a while.

Man Killer, on the ride back from town, told Colt about the conversation with Long-Legged Bear. They decided to break camp at daybreak and hide in a grove of trees just behind the livery stable, where they could watch for Buck Fuller's return.

The next morning, when Man Killer awakened shortly after dawn, he saw that Colt already had the horses saddled and the pack saddles on the horse. They needed only to break camp and pack the few remaining items. Colt was not around, so Man Killer assumed he was off hunting for a meal. The Nez Percé decided to relieve his bladder, so he stepped over under the cottonwood closest to the fire and started urinating. As soon as he started, a rope dropped down over his body and tightened around his ankles. Man Killer was immediately jerked up into the air. He saw Colt slide down past him as he jumped out of the tree, holding the other end of the rope. It all happened so quickly that the urine went all over Man Killer's pants and shirt while he was upside-down. He started swinging back and forth and could hear nothing but the loud laughter of Chris Colt.

"Let me down!" he yelled.

Colt laughed heartily and lowered his upside-down *compadre* to the ground. Man Killer looked down at his trousers and at the lower part of his shirt.

Chris said simply, "Better get some dry clothes on. We need to get to town," and then, with just a slight touch of sarcasm in his voice, he added, "mighty Nez Percé scout."

Colt walked over to the fire and pulled a burning brand out to light his cigarette. He sat on a log smoking while a very angry and embarrassed Man Killer changed clothes. Suddenly the young man stopped short. He realized that he had become the brunt of his own braggadocio, and he began laughing at himself. He finally finished changing and walked over to Colt and shook hands.

"Better eat some bacon and biscuits there," Colt said with a friendly gesture toward the food. "We have to go."

Late that afternoon, the livery stable owner rode up driving a large freighter wagon loaded with bales of alfalfa. Buck Fuller followed him in another wagon. While the two men unloaded the two wagons, Colt and Man Killer struck their lookout camp in the trees.

Chris had explained, "No sense making the

stable owner have to do the work of two men. We'll let them get the wagons unloaded.''

Man Killer was concerned, because Colt seemed like himself. They now watched one of the men involved in killing Colt's wife, and Chris was acting like they were going to ride down and make a simple arrest.

After the two wagons were unloaded, the stable owner and Buck sat down on a bench outside the stable and lit corncob pipes. Colt and Man Killer mounted up and slowly rode into town, keeping the stable between them and the two men until they were right at the corner. There they dismounted.

When they stepped around the corner, the corncob pipe literally dropped from Buck's mouth. The stable owner saw the look on Buck's face and the look of sheer hatred on Colt's as he stood there, hands hovering over both guns.

Teeth clenched, Colt said, ''Buck Fuller, you yellow cur, I am U.S. Deputy Marshal Chris Colt, and I am here to arrest you for the cold-blooded murder of Mrs. Shirley Colt and the attempted kidnapping of four children. You can hang for those crimes, or you can save us all a lot of trouble right now. You're packing iron. What's your decision?''

The stable owner was a middle-aged man

with a balding head and a plump little wife of twenty-two years. He sprang away from Buck Fuller and slammed his back up against the building. Apologetically, he said, "Marshal, I had no idea."

Colt said, "We figured that, mister. You're in no trouble. Just stay out of this."

"Yes, sir. I would have no party with a man who kills women."

Yet Colt's anger was cooling, disarmed by the look on Buck Fuller's face. Man Killer had told him what Long-Legged Bear had said, that Buck was simpleminded, and Chris could see that. His shoulders slumped a little and he rose out of the gunfighter's crouch. Nonetheless, Colt's right hand flashed down and came out with a cocked .45.

Colt said, "Slowly with the left hand, unbuckle your gun belt and let it drop."

Buck carefully complied.

Colt said, "Now, both hands, grab a couple of handfuls of cloud."

Buck seemed puzzled by that statement, but he reached skyward.

Colt said, "Man Killer, put the manacles on him."

Man Killer complied. Then Colt holstered his gun.

Chris said, "Mister, his partner is not far from here, and we would appreciate it if this arrest was kept quiet. We don't want him to know we are coming."

"No problem, Marshal," the man said fearfully. "My mouth is shut."

Colt said, "I'll take him and Hawk back to the trees, and you run down and tell the sheriff. Tell him we have to take him back to the deputy U.S. marshal in Cheyenne to hold for us until we return."

Man Killer gave Colt a queer look, hesitating. He didn't want to leave Colt alone with one of his wife's killers.

Colt finally said, "He has manacles on. He has them on his thinking, too. You know me when I have made up my mind. Your words earlier at the ranch hit me like a runaway train. I represent the law. Shirley used to tell me that all the time—this job was more important work for the country than scouting was."

Man Killer relaxed and smiled. He turned and walked quickly toward the marshal's office. Chris grabbed Hawk's reins and mounted up on War Bonnet. "He ride a horse in here?"

The livery stable owner said, "Yes, sir. I'll saddle him for ya right quick."

The man did so, and Colt instructed Fuller to

mount up. They went into the trees behind the town, and Man Killer returned minutes later. The three of them headed out for Cheyenne, bypassing the town. Colt didn't really want to take all the time to go to Cheyenne and return, but there was just no other way. He did not want to trust the safekeeping of Buck Fuller to a regular town marshal or county sheriff.

Man Killer was greatly relieved at Colt's decision and admired him even more. He knew that Colt had desperately wanted Buck Fuller to try to draw on him back in town, but he was glad that Buck hadn't.

After several miles the Indian deputy said to his friend, "I once saw a she-bear charge a man in my tribe who got too close to her cubs. The mighty bear was with her two cubs fishing for salmon. I was high on a bluff and could see a man of my band approach on a trail. He was going to catch fish traps, and I wanted to warn him but was too far away. I could only watch. The bear smelled the man and dropped on all fours and started toward him even before he walked around the bend. When he saw her, she stood on her hind legs and charged him. First, she sent the cubs up a tree. He backed away quickly, and she charged forward, but when she saw that he was backing away, she stopped. She then watched him and returned to her cubs, but before she called out to them, 'Come down my children. We are safe now,' she stopped at a small aspen tree and bit it."

Colt said, "Bit it?"

Man Killer said, "She bit it and growled, then started hitting the tree and biting the tree, over and over until it was no longer a tree. It became many leaves and pieces of wood on the ground. The bear was angry, very angry, but it did not continue to attack the man. She had to return to her cubs. That was her duty, but the man from my tribe was always more careful from then on to watch before he approached areas like that, so he would not upset a mother and her cubs. He learned his lesson, and the mother did her duty, and she did not have to kill him, and maybe get killed, too, doing that only because she was angry. For if she did, her cubs would have no mother anymore, just because she was too angry and did not do her duty."

Colt rode for a while before replying. When he did, he was grinning. "You know, little brother, it surprises me that you came from the tribe of Chief Joseph. You sure aren't much of a talker."

Man Killer chuckled, and they kept on southeast.

Buck Fuller never spoke the whole time until the morning before they rode into Cheyenne.

Before breaking camp on that last day, he said, "Suh, Marshal Colt. I is very sorry 'bout 'yo wife. She seemed a fine woman, an' I din't nevah wann have no truck wif sech as thet, but ah did, so's now I'll hang fer it. But anyways, suh, I is very sorry. I din't touch her nohow."

Colt nodded. "If you're really sorry, tell me where Aramus Randall is hiding out."

Buck said, "Suh, he was my pappy's frien' an' I hates what he done, but I cain't tell ya. Ah'm sorry, suh, but I jest cain't tell ya. He saved my pappy's life."

Colt simply said, "Okay," and continued striking camp.

Man Killer smiled to himself.

They rode into Cheyenne, where Colt turned the prisoner over to a federal deputy. The man promised Colt that Fuller would be held safely until Colt returned to transport him to Denver.

The man who had sneaked up on Chris Colt while he was attending to his natural requirements was named Jasper Coghill. A two-bit robber, he'd come out West from New York City seven years earlier, and nowadays he held up weary travelers he would sneak up on along different roadways. Most of the time he only got a few dollars, normally from cowboys riding the grub line and looking for ranch jobs. What ruined him was during his first summer out West, he'd held up a Dutch-born cattle rancher in Montana. The man was too cheap to take a train and had just sold a herd and was carrying three thousand dollars on him. Jasper was ruined by that good luck, especially when he went through all the money in less than a month. He did buy himself a nice-looking long-legged chestnut thoroughbred with four white stockings. He was sure that the horse would help him outdistance any posse that might pursue him. Unfortunately, Jasper found out a week after he bought the horse that the steed was suffering from nevicular disease. Within a few more days the horse could not even walk anymore without a severe limp. Jasper was so angry, he pulled out his pistol and shot the horse through the head and left him lying in front of a watering trough.

Jasper knew who had captured him, and he listened closely to the words exchanged between Colt and Man Killer. He had seen the man they spoke of because he was a fellow outlaw. Although he was essentially harmless and had killed nobody, while Aramus Randall was a cold-blooded killer, still in all, Jasper was privy to information that somebody like Chris Colt would never hear. Jasper could drink a beer in saloons and hear freely spoken conversations about murder and robbery, while an ordinary citizen might enter that same saloon and the conversation would be about weather, range conditions, and normal gossip.

With a big reward in mind and plenty of time to kill, Jasper spent his jail time standing on his bunk and staring through the bars of his window in Jackson. He was watching for the mean-looking brown-skinned gunfighter to come to town, as he had done before. Aramus Randall had the most haunting, scary eyes he had ever seen, and just looking at the man sent a chill through his body. That did not matter to Jasper, however, for he wanted money.

While Colt and Man Killer were in Cheyenne, Jasper's vigil paid off. Aramus Randall, receiving his paycheck from the mine he was working in at the base of the Grand Tetons, rode into town to get drunk and seek out the latest information on the Colts from his compatriot Buck Fuller.

As Aramus rode by the jail, Jasper started whistling, but Aramus at first didn't hear him.

When he finally did look around and make eye contact, the marshal walked into the cell block and yelled at Jasper, "Here, you, get away from that window. Who were you whistling at?"

Jasper said, "My horse. It looked like somebody was just riding down the street on my horse! What the hell d'ya do, sell him?"

The marshal said, "What's it look like?"

Jasper lied, "A dark bay gelding. His name's Dandy."

The marshal ran out of the office. Of course, several brown horses were going up and down the street in both directions. The marshal set off to identify them. This gave Jasper a chance to run back to the window. Yet Aramus was nowhere in sight. He planted himself at the window, frowning. He'd wait all night if he had to.

Aramus went straightaway to the stable and looked around for Buck. His strict instructions to the half-wit were to remain at the stable and only leave if he was instructed to for his work. He was not to drink or get into any kind of trouble, but was to buy his lunches at saloons where he could listen to gossip, much of which was about famous gunfighters such as Colt.

Aramus rode behind the livery stable and checked the outbuilding, but no Buck, so he rode back around to the front. He dismounted and went into the livery stable. The owner was sitting by Long-Legged Bear, both repairing harness.

Aramus said, "Way is yo helpah, Buck Fuller? I dint see him nowhere roun heah."

The stable master seemed nervous, Aramus thought, and it bothered him some, but it could just be his way, he thought.

The man, heeding his instructions from Man Killer, said, "He left several days ago. Told me to tell anyone looking for him that he went to Georgia, but I heard him talking with some Mexican feller about going to Texas. They were talking about making some big money, but I sure couldn't see Buck making big money. You know what I mean?"

Aramus gritted his teeth and said, "I know."

Angry—and a little confused Buck would do this—he mounted up and rode back up the street. He heard the whistle again and spotted the yahoo in the window of the jail. He rode down the alley to the window and pulled up by Jasper.

"Make it fas,' mistah," he said. "I don' wanna git nabbed for 'tempted jailbreak."

Jasper said, "Mr. Randall, I have information for you if you'll pay me."

Aramus said, "Go to hell."

He reined up and was wheeling around when

Jasper said, "It's about Chris Colt. That's who put me in here."

Aramus turned back to the window and said, "Tell me fast an' I'll give you a hunnerd bucks and break ya outta jail."

Jasper told him why Colt was in the area and how he was going after Buck and Aramus both. He related everything he could think of that had happened from the time he ran into Colt.

Jasper smiled, saying, "That's all I can think of, Mr. Randall. How are you gonna get me out of here?"

Aramus laughed, saying, "Is yo stupid? I ain't gittin' yo sorry ass outta dere. Thanks, dummy."

Jasper went into a rage as Aramus rode away. "You black nigger! I'll kill you when I get out of here!"

Aramus wheeled his horse and rode up to the cell bars again and grinned. "What do yo call me, boy? Wanna hit me? Come on."

He stuck his chin almost up to the bar, which invited the enraged Jasper to take a punch. As the fist came out between the bars, the chin was pulled back. Aramus grabbed Jasper's wrist with his hand. He then yanked the arm sideways, snapping it between the bars. Jasper squealed in pain. A knife flashed in the killer's hand, and he drove it through the bars and into

Jasper's Adam's apple. Aramus slashed the blade to the left and twisted it. There was a loud gurgling sound as blood sprayed through the bars all over the face, arm, and chest of the former slave. He laughed it off, though, and spun his horse around, wiping the blade on his pant leg.

Aramus rode down the alley and behind the buildings on Main Street. He returned to the livery stable and tied his horse in the rear. The owner, sitting there speaking with Long-Legged Bear, was now repairing a saddle, while the old Crow still worked on trace harness. Long-Legged Bear started to speak when something flashed by him and his immediate reaction was that it was a bird swooping by, but a knife appeared in the stablemaster's chest with a loud thud. Long-Legged Bear turned his head and looked into the evil eyes of Aramus Randall. The killer thought the Indian was crazy because he suddenly started singing a song in Crow, repeating many of the same words over and over. He didn't know that the old man was actually singing his death song. The warrior had seen the look in Aramus's eyes and was certain he was about to die. Aramus was not a warrior, like many brave Crows and enemies that Long-

Legged Bear had known over the years. He enjoyed killing and was simply evil.

The owner of the stable fell over backward, his chest soaked in blood from the fatal heart wound.

Aramus grinned and explained, "He lied ta me." He stepped on the man's chest with both feet and pulled the knife free. He wiped it on the stablemaster's pants and turned for the back door. "See ya, Chief."

Long-Legged Bear, with a speed nobody had ever seen around town, ran to the back door and watched the man turn the horse toward the nearby mountains and ride. He quickly ran back inside the livery stable and dumped grain out of feed buckets and set them upside-down behind the stable. He then started forking bedding straw into a big pile over the buckets.

He went back inside and then went to get the marshal.

Colt and Man Killer sat in the café watching the old Crow brave wolfing down his steak and potatoes. Chris Colt had never seen any one person consume so much sugar in one cup of coffee.

The man looked up at Colt between bites and

said, "I have heard that you believe in the Great Mystery that white men call God. Is this true?"

Chris said, "Yes, I do."

"Tell me, Colt, do you know of the evil spirit you call Satan?"

Chris said, "Yes."

The Crow said, "I have looked into the eyes of your Satan."

Colt said, "That bad, huh?"

Long-Legged Bear said, "My winter count has grown long, and I have seen many men and many things."

Colt said, "I believe that."

"I have never looked into the eyes of a man like this one."

"Which way did he go? Did you see?"

Long-Legged Bear said, "After we eat and smoke, I will show you."

Man Killer said, "Should we not go now, Colt?"

Chris said, "No, it's been two days since he killed the stablemaster and took off. We need to rest the horses and ourselves before we go. We'll track him down."

After they ate and smoked, Long-Legged Bear took them to the stable and started forking the pile of bedding straw off the buckets. Man Killer gave Colt a funny look, as if questioning the old

Crow's sanity. He finally got the four buckets uncovered and sat down on one of the ones he had turned over. Colt knew Indians well enough to let the man entertain himself and play this one out.

"Those cigars are good," Long-Legged Bear said, looking at Colt with a smile.

Chris grinned and gave the old man a cigarillo and a light. Long-Legged Bear offered the first four puffs of smoke to each compass point and then took a long, slow drag.

He said, "You want Long-Legged Bear to paint picture of the trail of your Satan?"

Colt said, "Of course."

"Long-Legged Bear knew you two soon come. I covered his tracks while he rode into trees yonder. There under buckets."

Colt and Man Killer smiled broadly. Where the straw pile had been were all four hoof tracks of the horse that Aramus Randall rode. The Crow could not have given Colt a greater gift. He and Man Killer committed the size, shape, and oddities of each hoofprint to memory. To them, it was like a longtime bank teller knowing his customers' signatures.

Colt and Man Killer both reached down into their pockets and dug out several double eagle twenty-dollar gold pieces each. They handed the money to the old man and patted him on the back.

Colt gave him a reward that meant even more. Long-Legged Bear knew that Chris Colt's first wife, the Lakotah of the Minniconjou tribe named Chantapeta and his first daughter, Winona, had been killed by a band of four renegade Crows, so Colt's words meant much to him.

Chris said, "The Crow are a mighty nation, and you have apparently been given much of the great wisdom of your people. No white man would have thought to cover those tracks for us, but you, in your wisdom, did."

Long-Legged Bear pointed at a distant tree line saying, "There across that meadow. See the two trees which are big brothers to the others?"

Colt said, "Yes."

The Crow said, "He passed between those trees. In that meadow there were many wapiti."

Colt smiled, patted the man on the back, and stuck a tin of cigarillos in the man's hand.

The lawmen had already checked their horses into the other livery stable, so they headed toward the hotel to get a pair of rooms. They would leave at first light, but now they would get a bath, shave, meal, and then sleep in feather beds.

*   *   *

Man Killer thought back to a big chase by a crooked deputy named Wolf Keeler. Keeler had falsely accused Man Killer of killing two men when in fact it was self-defense. When Man Killer realized that he would be killed in jail, he decided he should escape.

Man Killer chuckled to himself as he recalled his jailbreak. The floor and wall of his cell had been concrete. He could not escape from within the cell, so he would have to wait for the lynch mob and take his chances with them. Or he would have to somehow trick Wolf Keeler into moving him out of the cell.

Man Killer searched every nook and cranny inside and outside of his cell for an idea, or for something he could use to help him. All he could find was an old dirty sock left under the bunk by a previous prisoner. Plus, the floor was covered with tiny pebbles and sand from deteriorating concrete.

A thought struck the young scout, and he grinned broadly. He grabbed the sock and dropped to his hands and knees, scraping the sand and tiny pebbles into it. When he saw movement out of the corner of his eye, he quickly sat back on the cot, holding his stomach. Wolf Keeler walked over to the cell carrying an

Don Bendell

Overland shotgun, a twelve-gauge double-barrel greener sawed off to about eighteen inches. It was loaded with double-ought buckshot.

"What the hell you doin,' red nigger?" the deputy asked.

Man Killer moaned and pointed at his stomach.

Wolf chuckled and said, "Aw, yer little tummy hurts 'cause yer so scared, ain't ya? Wait a bit more, boy, 'cause they're damned shore comin' to stretch yer sorry red neck tonight. Ya ready ta bring up yer supper? Go 'head. I'll make ya lick it up off the floor." He grinned harshly. "Ya know, sometimes when a man hangs, his eyeballs pop clean outta his head, an' he goes in his drawers. Bet it all happens ta you, nigger boy."

Man Killer just moaned and dropped to the floor. Wolf laughed and walked back to the office. Sitting down behind his desk, he started looking through a stack of wanted posters. Man Killer curled up on the floor, and shielding what he was doing from sight, started scraping more sand and gravel into the sock. He kept this up until the sock was filled up and packed solid.

Next, Man Killer clutched the sock firmly in his right hand and held it between his legs. He started writhing on the floor and pretended to vomit. He made horrible retching sounds, and finally the deputy walked back over to the cell, again wearing his evil grin.

"I warned ya, boy. Good 'n' sick now, huh? This is awright. It's plumb awright," he said, "Now, what I want ya to do, nigger, is ta—"

Boom! Man Killer straightened up like a snake striking, and that sock came from between his legs. His right arm shot out at the lawman's face, and the makeshift blackjack hit Wolf Keeler right between the eyes with a loud thud. The man's nose was smashed flat, and blood spurted in every direction. He tottered for a moment, before his eyes rolled back in his head and his legs folded underneath him. As the man slumped forward, Man Killer caught the deputy by the lapels and pulled him against the bars.

Dropping the sock, Man Killer caught the shotgun with his right hand and pulled it between the bars. He quickly stripped off the man's belt and holster and pulled it into the cell with him in case anyone barged in the door. He searched the man's pockets but couldn't find the keys. He was starting to lose heart when he saw something almost sticking out of the right boot. It was a boot knife in a sheath, and around the handle was a little chain with a large key attached. He pulled it out and tried it in the steel door. The key turned and the tumbler clicked. The mighty steel cage door released. Man Killer felt his heart skip a beat. Smiling, he dragged the injured deputy into the cell and bound his hands behind his back and gagged him as well.

Brodie Pace worked for Preston Millard, a crooked mine owner that Colt and Man Killer had put out of business, and he was the one who had Keeler and others in his pocket. Brodie's job this night was simple; he'd been given a wad of bills by Millard and told to buy drinks for men and whip them into a frenzied lynch mob. From the saloon Brodie brought two dozen angry, drunken men to the jail, carrying torches and lanterns. He held a stout hemp rope, which someone had tied into a hangman's noose. Arrangements had already been made with Wolf Keeler to drag out the young Indian. They would simply string him up from the nearest tree.

Brodie waved with his arm, yelling, "Come on, boys. Let's string up that redskin murderer!"

When he stepped inside the jail, though, he was surprised to see the deputy's chair empty.

He yelled, "Wolf!"

To that shout, he was greeted with a muffled sound from the cell. He found Wolf Keeler, with broken nose and face covered in blood, gagged, and his arms up over his head, wrists tied to the bars of the small cell window. His ankles were tied, with the bed sheet, to the frame of the cot, and he seemed to be in great pain.

Brodie couldn't figure out what had happened to the Indian. He'd had the outside of the jail watched all night for any possibility of escape. The mob looked all around the jail, but there was no sign of Man Killer. Finally, one of the men hollered for Brodie and Wolf, who was now free. As they ran into the office, the man slid the large desk to the side and showed them where three of the floorboards in the office had been pried loose. They had been blocked from view by the massive desk.

"Son of a . . ." Brodie exclaimed. "Quick, outside! He couldn't have gotten very far."

Outside, they spotted nothing moving but a single buckboard with two drunken men driving it back to their ranch.

Brodie hollered at the men, "Here, you two, hold up there!"

The men reined the wagon, and the crowd rushed up to it, leaving the drunks quite bewildered. Wolf Keeler, pinching his nostrils, looked over the side rails, and one man jumped up into the back of the wagon, looking under a tarp and even under the buckboard seat to insure Man Killer was not there.

One of the drunks giggled at his friend and said to Brodie, "I kin see you boys admire this wagon a lot, but it ain't fer sale."

Brodie said quietly, "Go on. You can go."

The second drunk found his friend's joke quite amusing and his raucous laughter echoed off the buildings in the deserted street as the two rode away. Wolf and Brodie were beside themselves with anger.

Minutes later, the wagon turned the corner and passed the livery stable. Underneath the slow-moving vehicle a shadow dropped to the ground, a knife in each hand. Man Killer's arms and legs ached from the exertion of hanging underneath the wagon, knives stuck into the wood and toes gripping the edges of the bottom of the floorboards.

Aramus had decided that he would be leaving the mine one day, and when he did, the paymaster's cashbox contents were going to go with him. When he took off out of Jackson, he decided that day had come. Aramus was thankful that the mine had closed down for two days after a cave-in, when two men on the graveyard shift had been crushed under several tons of quartzite.

Aramus climbed up on some rocks and watched the mine for activity for an hour before he rode down. He headed directly for the mine office. He entered and found the paymaster behind his desk.

The paymaster said, "Oh, howdy, Randall. Vhat is it yo are doing here dis mornink?"

Aramus grinned and drew his six-shooter. "Ah done come to hep yo out. Yo given me dat batch a money ya keeps in thet safe, an' yo won't die."

"Yiminy," the paymaster growled, "ya yust can't come in here an' hold me up. Da men'll be comin' outta da mine soon, I'll bet."

Aramus said, "Yo right shoulder."

The paymaster said, "Huh?"

With a flash of his hands, Aramus did a border shift, tossing his pistol from the right to the left hand. His right hand went down to the back of his gun belt and swung forward with a blade in it. All in one motion the arm whipped forward and the knife spun over once in the air and stuck in the paymaster's right shoulder. The paymaster screamed and grabbed the knife to pull it out.

Aramus said, "Yo eye."

The paymaster moaned, "Vhat?"

Aramus said, "I tole yo where ah was gwine ta stick dat knife. Now I has said da next one goes in you eye. Now gimme da money in a poke. Do it quick an ah won't kills ya."

Still moaning in pain, the paymaster opened his strongbox and filled a bank bag with bills. He handed it to a grinning Aramus, who reached up and pulled his knife free and sheathed it.

"Now leave," the paymaster said bravely.

Aramus said, "Say, does yo and yo wife still live in dat shack up on da hill?"

The paymaster replied, "Yah, so vhat if ve do?"

Aramus said, "Yo is ugly, but she be a purty little thing. Ah always wonnert what was under dem clothes."

In a flash Aramus buried the knife in the paymaster's right eye. Before he had time to scream in agony, he fell dead. Aramus looked in the bank bag and chuckled then he looked out the window and eyed the shack on the hill.

Oddly enough, the miners in the skeleton crew were working so hard to dig out the bodies that it was a day and a half before the bodies of the paymaster and his wife were discovered.

One of their men immediately was sent to Jackson to wire the county sheriff.

On the way there he ran into Chris Colt and Man Killer. Seeing their badges, he knew who they were right away.

"Marshal, Marshal," he said. "Are you Marshal Colt and are you Man Killer?"

Man Killer answered with a nod.

The miner went on, "Pleased to meet you both, gentlemen. We just had two killings and a rape and a robbery at our mine, Marshal. It's about fifteen miles north."

"Negro feller? Mean eyes? Carries several knives?" Colt said.

The miner replied, "That sounds like Aramus Randall. Both killings were done with a knife, but nobody saw anything. A couple of men said it might be Aramus when they saw the knife wounds. He was always throwing knifes, and I never seen better."

Colt said, "Let's get going."

When they arrived at the mine, Colt and Man Killer combed the area for sign and saw Randall's tracks leading away to the north. They told everyone that it was indeed Aramus Randall and promised that he would hang.

The two men rode north, following a trail of a man with the eyes of Satan.

* * *

Aramus Randall was upset. He had over two thousand dollars in cash, but he had no place to go. He knew that Colt would be on his trail, and he would have to use every trick in his book to shake him.

The outlaw headed north along the western slope of the Grand Tetons. At first he didn't worry about the trail he was leaving. He wanted to get some miles under him. Then he would start covering his back trail more carefully. He had learned some ruses and figured something would work. The mountains to the north were plenty rough, and he was not going to make it easy.

Colt and Man Killer came upon a tubular plant that was red, orange, and had brownish leaves. Colt dismounted and pulled up several of the plants and placed them in his saddlebags. He remounted, and they continued on.

Man Killer said, "You like the Indian turnip?"

Chris Colt said, "You know, I made pain and headache powder from it when I was in Kansas and used it in a poultice with bear grease and yarrow to treat my wounds. It helped a great deal and really helped me deal with a lot of pain."

That first day Aramus rode his horse into a

real lather and then decided to make camp for the night. He rubbed the horse down good and made sure there was plenty of grass for him to graze on. Without eating, he rolled up in his bedroll and fell asleep.

The next morning he made a large breakfast with the little bit of food he had and decided he'd have to start trying to hide his trail. He also decided to make booby traps as Colt's son had done to his gang.

He had heard that Colt had killed Will Sawyer in a gunfight in the Yellowstone, and he headed in the direction it was located. He knew Colt wouldn't figure out why, though, because it had been a national park for over a decade and had become very popular with dudes from back East. This was what Aramus wanted. It would be obvious that he was indeed headed for the Yellowstone, but his intention was to turn almost due south and head back toward Colorado.

He started riding up the middle of a north-south creek, which would not follow an average tracker, let alone Colt and Man Killer. Aramus Randall had some very definite plans. First, he would make it south to the Flaming Gorge area at Green River. From there, he would head east for a ways until he was north of Fort Collins and head back down into Colorado at that point.

He rode for miles in the creek, hoping it might cover his trail somewhat, especially if it rained either there or higher up where the water would turn the creek muddy brown. What he did not realize was that Man Killer and Chris would simply get on each side of the stream when they found he entered it and would keep riding until one of them came across the tracks where he egressed the waterway.

They had not reached the creek yet, but when they did they would simply move much faster than Aramus, who would be greatly slowed down moving through the water. Occasionally, they would go into the stream and check for rocks that would have been scuffed by horse-shoes, just to insure that he had not doubled back in the creek. All in all, though, once Colt and Man Killer started following the waterway, they would make up for quite a bit of lost time. When Aramus finally left the creek, he was still heading north, but he stopped and covered the tracks he left with grass, leaves, and sticks. That, too, would not fool the two trackers behind him, but he didn't know that. He could only hope.

Chris and Man Killer kept on following the easy trail north, and came to his overnight camp. They dismounted and rested and watered the horses. While Man Killer made a small fire and a meal a short distance away, Chris Colt got down on his hands and knees and scoured every square inch of the killer's campsite. He carefully examined every track, every indentation in the ground, food scraps, even counting how many cigarette butts there were. When he finished, he rejoined Man Killer.

Colt said, "He made one meal. Had sourdough biscuits, corn, bacon, and coffee. Looks like he didn't make any kind of camp. Just ate, rolled up, and went to sleep. He must have slept long, too, judging by how much grass the horse ate and all the tracks he left all over the meadow."

Man Killer said, "Soon, I think, he will try to start covering his trail. Do you think so?"

Colt said, "Yep. Makes sense. He probably figured he should put some distant between himself and the mine first."

As they rode farther, Man Killer looked over at his silent partner. He had been looking ahead quite often, a distant look on his face.

Man Killer said, "Great Scout, you think of the Land of Many Smokes and of Will Sawyer."

Colt said, "Yes, I wonder if he is leading us there."

"I wonder, too," Man Killer added. "Many people go there now to see the geysers and to camp. It is not somewhere I would run to if being chased. Many years ago I would, but not now."

Aramus had one more trick up his sleeve. He got off his horse and took his blanket roll out. He used a knife to cut off the end of it, then cut it into four patches. He put these over his horse's hooves and tied them around the ankles with leather cords. Once he took off on the horse again, he looked back. He could barely see the tracks left behind. A big smile spread across his face.

Colt and Man Killer found where he entered the stream and smiled at each other. Man Killer went across the stream and paralleled Colt and the far bank as the two men took off at a fast trot. They had to finally give up because of dark and make camp along the creek.

The next morning, the lawmen were on the trail an hour before Aramus got up. By high noon, they had discovered where he left the stream and almost laughed at his feeble attempts to cover his trail. What they did not know was that he was now crossing over a high ridge miles to the north and could see them as tiny dots in the valley in the distance. He crossed over to the next valley and headed due south.

Before long, Colt and Man Killer found where he had stopped and put the pieces of cloth on each hoof. The two men chuckled as they looked at his prints where he kneeled and where he lifted the horse's hooves. They also found bits of thread from the cloth he placed on the hooves.

They mounted up and continued north, watching a little more closely, but the cloth pads did not hide the trail. They found a place eventually where he had run across somebody with a smaller horse, and the two had dismounted and talked for a while, each smoking a cigarette. The other rider continued west, and Aramus kept on to the north, getting closer and closer to the Yellowstone. A short ride from the south entrance to the big park, the two men had to make camp again.

The next morning, Chris Colt dreaded the ride ahead of him. They would be going into Yellowstone National Park, the biggest tourist attraction in the West, but what bothered Colt was that everything about the place reminded him of one of his greatest battles and of the woman he loved. They had barely entered the park and crested over the first rise when they spotted the horse they had followed for so many miles.

The two men looked at each other and spurred their horses down the hill, drawing their carbines on the way.

They were soon overtaking the rider, and Colt hollered at him, "Rein up! Grab the sky now! You're under arrest!"

The man stuck his hands up in the air and said, "What did I do, Marshal? What did I do?"

As Colt pulled abreast, he found himself looking at a slender, white-skinned brown-haired man. This couldn't be right. "Where did you get that horse, mister?"

The man said, "I run into an old Negro boy yesterday south a here with this big, pretty thoroughbred. He told me he had to get somewhere fast and asked if I wanted to trade even, saddles and all. All I had to do was grab my fishing gear and saddlebags. I fish the Yellowstone River all the time. I was just riding my old Morgan nag, so I traded, sure enough. The horse ain't stole, is it?"

Colt saw the fishing pole and tackle bag lashed onto the side of the horse. He scowled deeply. "Not that I know of."

Man Killer said, "Why did you trade for a horse with cloth around his hooves?"

The man said, "He told me that he had to leave those on, because the doctor put medicine on the rags. Something like laudanum because the horse got caught in quicksand and strained his muscles in his ankles. He said he'd be okay in two days."

Colt and Man Killer frowned at each other. They were both the biggest fools in the world.

Man Killer said, "We have been tricked by a man who could not hide his back trail if he had wings like an angel and could fly over the clouds."

Colt turned his horse and said, "Come on, we have some riding to do."

They headed back south, backtracking to the spot where the men had swapped horses. After several hours they arrived and this time headed west. The Morgan's tracks were fairly easy to recognize. The horse wore size aught shoes, which was fairly normal, but his right front foot toed in a little bit.

The usually unflappable Colt was furious. "I can't believe I was so stupid," he fumed as they rode along.

Man Killer said, "You were not. You were a man, like all other men. Sometimes you make mistakes and so do I."

Colt said nothing but continued pushing War Bonnet in silence. After several hours of alternating between a slow canter and a fast trot, Man Killer felt it was time to speak again.

He said, "I remember when I was a boy, a great man told me one time how he rode a horse hard when he was young. He was coming home from the Great War of the White Men, and he rode the horse to death. He told me he learned then that you must always protect your horse, because they are but dumb animals which will die for you if you wish."

Colt looked over at Man Killer and grinned. "We ought to take a break for lunch."

This time Colt fetched the firewood and made the meal while Man Killer unsaddled the horses and let them rest, water, and graze. First, all three horses, soaking wet from the hard riding, took turns having a nice roll in a dry sandy spot. The two men relaxed and ate.

Smoking afterward, Man Killer said, "We both made a mistake, but it bothers you more because this man killed Shirley. You must relax. You must act like we are trailing any other outlaw, or we will make more mistakes."

They continued south, and after four days of hard riding, they realized he had headed to Green River. War Bonnet and Hawk had already proven that they would run down the best of horses, but Morgan horses were noted for stamina. The only good thing was that the trail of the murderer was getting fresher all the time. "Soon," Colt said to Man Killer. "Soon we'll run him down."

They were only a few hours behind Aramus when more bad luck befell them. Aramus had been riding along outside Green River when he saw a line stretching far out east and west. At first he thought it was a road, but then realized it was the Union Pacific Railway. Next, Aramus saw a plume of smoke coming far out to the west—a train heading eastbound. He rode fast toward the highest part of the grade off to the east and waited there for the approaching freight. While the horse took a blow, Aramus untied his saddlebags and bedroll and tied them on his back like a pack. As the train approached the grade, it started slowing, and Aramus started running his horse parallel to the tracks. He watched for a boxcar with an open door. There was one about halfway back, so he paced his horse for that one. The surefooted Morgan got him up next to the open door, and Aramus leaned over out of the saddle, trying to grab the door. No matter how hard he tried, though, he couldn't stretch far enough.

Just then a tall, slim cowboy appeared in the

doorway, a gold-toothed grin on his face. He leaned out of the door and held his hand out. Aramus flashed an evil smile and nodded. Grabbing the man's hand, he launched himself from the saddle. With the cowboy pulling at the same time, Aramus easily flew into the boxcar.

The cowboy's grin disappeared immediately as Aramus got to his feet and a bowie knife flashed. Into the cowboy's stomach it plunged, over and over. Aramus yanked and the man flew out onto the roadbed. "Thanks, pardner."

Aramus calmly wiped his blade and checked the cowboy's saddlebags. He took what food he wanted, some bullets, matches, tobacco, a brand-new tin coffee cup, and a red bib shirt. He then tossed the rest out of the door, then admired his new saddle. He removed his dirty bloody shirt and replaced it with the new one and tossed his own away.

Less than an hour later Colt and Man Killer approached the tracks and rode along, following the horse tracks for miles. They came across the body of the dead cowboy and finally spotted the Morgan horse a mile ahead. The two men overtook the horse and unsaddled him, turning him loose.

This time Colt remained calm. Turning his

horse back toward the west, he said, "Come on. We'll ride back to Rock Springs and telegraph the marshal in Cheyenne. It's about two hundred and sixty miles to Cheyenne, so he'll have plenty of time to get a reception party ready."

Aramus had the feeling that Colt was hot on his heels. Plus, he started worrying about somebody else maybe finding the cowboy's body along the tracks and wiring ahead. He looked out one door of the boxcar and saw nothing but open country. He walked over to the other door and grinned. Every few seconds a telegraph pole flashed by him. He drew his gun, laid it across his left arm, and aimed at the telegraph wire. He squeezed off a shot and cursed. He'd missed. He fired again and a third time. This time Aramus was rewarded with the sight of the wire snapping and falling to the ground.

He would wait a few hours and shoot the wire in another spot, just in case someone made it out from Rock Springs in time to repair the break and send a wire from there. Aramus felt good. He laid down to rest, his head on his newly acquired saddle and took a nap.

Chris and Man Killer left the telegraph office and headed back to the railroad ticket office.

Colt said, "Look, if there's no eastbound train until tomorrow morning, how about one of those repair cars they use on the tracks?"

"Naw, Marshal," the man said, "Ah'm shore sorry. Thay's nothin' ya kin do till mahnin. Might tas well git ya a room. Try the Rock Spring Hotel. Good vittles, too."

Colt sighed and smiled bravely, saying, "Thank you, sir."

CHAPTER 11

Family

They both smiled and signed pieces of paper for the man and remounted their horses, looking for a livery stable. At least the three horses and the two men would get some good food and a good night's rest again. The next day, they had tickets aboard the morning eastbound. They would get off at Cheyenne and pick up their prisoner and transport him to Denver by railroad and get him tried as soon as possible.

Because they were witnesses and because of the circumstances, the judge had Buck Fuller appearing before him two days later. The dense young man pled guilty, figuring there was no use arguing or pleading his innocence. The judge probably would have sentenced Buck to death by hanging, but Colt asked if he could speak. The judge allowed it and Colt and Man Killer both asked the judge to punish Buck but spare his life. Buck was sentenced to a life term at Old Max, the state maximum security penitentiary in Canon City, so the two men were told to escort him to the prison.

On the way down to Canon City, the shackled and manacled prisoner thanked them both for asking for his life. He also apologized to Colt again for what had happened to his wife and children.

Aramus Randall could gloat that he had outwitted the legendary lawman and tracker, Chris Colt. But he still could not abide the fact that he had been outwitted and tricked repeatedly by a seven-, but now, eight-year-old boy.

The security around the Coyote Run Ranch was very tough, with rough-looking cowboys with rifles posted everywhere it seemed. Aramus didn't care. He would wait for the right opportunity to present itself, and he would strike. After all, he had outwitted the greatest living tracker in the country. He was certain he could outwit a few guards making forty a month.

He rode around the perimeter up in the hills under the cover of trees and watched with his spyglass. Then he noticed Texas Creek running through the middle of the sprawling mountain ranch. Ten feet wide in some places, it ran fast and varied from knee-deep to five or six feet. He could conceivably start upstream and crawl down through the cutbacks, past the guards, and sneak into the big house after nightfall. Charley Colt, he had found out, was occupying the big main house with her two daughters and the two children of Chris Colt. She or one of her daughters would occasionally go to the newer smaller house not too far away, to get things such as clothing. He assumed that must be her house, and she was occupying her brother's to watch his children.

Tex Westchester several times he spotted, the old man who had knocked him off the porch. If he got a chance, he would take him out, too. The large Colt brother he had heard about, the half-Negro, seemed to be gone, and his house looked like nobody was in it. Though he didn't know, Joshua had to deliver two bulls to a ranch out in High Park, planning to return in several days.

He would lie in wait just west of the big house in the stream. Then he thought, no, that would be too cold. He would instead crawl out under some bushes right next to the stream. He could easily see the house from there. After dark, he would inch forward on his belly—except the big wolf would be a problem. It was staying on the big veranda and escorted anybody from the family who left the big house and walked anywhere during the day. Then an idea struck him. He would sneak in as planned, then at dusk he would make light whistles to attract the wolf and stick him with one of his bowie knives when he got close enough for a sure throw.

Chris Colt was only forty-four miles away in Canon City, checking Buck Fuller in as the newest inmate at the Colorado State Maximum Security Prison, built opposite the hotel with the great mineral hot baths that Man Killer and Chris Colt liked to enjoy when they were in town. Right on the Arkansas River, they only needed to look a hundred yards or so to see the big stone facility at the base of the end of the big Hogback, the long sharp ridge overlooking town to the west. Just a few hundred yards downstream from where the Grand Canyon of the Arkansas, which some were calling the Royal Gorge, ended, and Grape Creek spilled into the mighty Arkansas River, the luxurious mineral hot baths were a sharp contrast to the infamous detention facility virtually a stone's throw away from them. Basically across the street, the River Road wound its way all the way through and past Salida and out west past Bent's Old Fort, where it became part of the Santa Fe Trail.

His plan set, Aramus Randall made his way down the stream and onto the ranch property. So far it had been easier than he thought it would be. The crystal-clear water was freezing cold, coming down out of glaciers in the mountain range. It took him most of the afternoon and some sore arms and legs from the crawling he had to do, but he found himself finally under the low bushes he had spotted. Tex and other cowboys passed by him, doing ranch work, never suspecting he was so close. His ears pricked up when he heard one of the younger ones challenging Tex and some others to a poker game in the bunkhouse after dark.

Finally, evening settled in. Tex went to the big house, less than one hundred paces away, right after supper, and apparently asked Charley if everything was okay. Aramus could tell by the body language that she had sent him off to have fun and not worry about her. When he walked by, Aramus saw that he was carrying a big slice of apple pie with steam coming off of it. Soon after, the poker game was obviously going on in earnest in the distant bunkhouse, judging by the hollers and cusswords.

Aramus thought about the incredible beauty of this Colt woman and the beauty of Shirley Colt. He decided that he had even had the opportunity to take Shirley Colt and enjoy her screaming in terror when he disrobed her and attacked her. He never got the chance. She was too much of a fighter, but this Charlotte Colt was wearing an apron and simple gingham dress, but the curves in it were so pronounced, she still looked more desirable than any dance hall beauty he had ever seen, no matter what they wore. Her long golden hair and stunning face were even impressive from that distance in the dimming light, when he saw her speaking with Tex. He got excited now imagining what she was going to look like underneath the apron and gingham dress and what she would look like screaming in abject terror, before he slit her throat. Then he imagined the little boy screaming as he slowly cut him to shreds, and the look on Colt's face when he knew the rest of his family had been killed by someone much mightier and tougher than he.

Drawing out a bowie knife, Aramus imitated the high-pitched, bleating sound of a dying rabbit. As he hoped, Kuli's ears stood up, and his nose tested the wind. He came forward eagerly toward the cries of the dying animal. Yet about ten feet from the bushes he stopped, growling and pacing back and forth in front of the undergrowth. Aramus knew he had to make a very good throw. He drew back and sent the knife spinning forward. The animal jumped at the last second, but still the blade caught him in mid-jump and sliced into his side. The wolf slumped to the ground, unmoving.

Aramus moved forward in a crouch, watching sharply for guards. He made it to the porch and up the steps, carefully. He crouched behind a porch swing. Slowly rising, he looked in the windows. Charlotte Colt was carrying a little girl up the stairs. The other ones apparently were already upstairs in their rooms. Randall crept around to the kitchen door and went in, locking it behind him. He tiptoed to the living room and locked that door, too. In his hand he carried his other bowie knife.

At the bottom of the long staircase, there was a foyer and a small coat closet. He hid within, not latching the door. Before long, she came down the stairs. Her beauty was even more stunning up close. He decided he would tie up all the children and take her in front of them before killing them all. He was excited thinking about the terror he would cause in all of them. He could not wait to slit the throat of the brat who had made him look like a fool in the mountains just west of the big house.

As Charley walked past the closet, he shot out, his left arm wrapping around her throat and the knife blade going up against her windpipe.

"Shh," he whispered, nipping on her neck with his teeth, "I'm gonna look at yer insides ef'n ya makes a peep. Understand?"

Charley said, "My husband's upstairs. He's cleaning his shotgun, and he'll be right down. If I were you, I'd take the money—it's in the cookie jar—and get out of here."

He chuckled quietly. "Who do you think I am? I done kilt yer sister-in-law. Now I'm back for you and the young uns. Yer brotha, the great tracker, the great lawman, he's still up in Wyoming ridin' aroun' and tryin' ta figger out where I am."

Keeping the knife at her throat, he grabbed Charley's breast with his free hand. "That's mighty fine."

Calming her near panic, Charley said, "I will cooperate with anything you want, but please leave the children out of this."

He said, "Naw, I ain't gonna do thet. Call them down here, now, an' ef'n ya don't, I'll jest take ya upstairs an start stabbin' 'em one by one.''

She hollered, "Children, come down here!" She yelled it as loud as she could, hoping that Tex might hear her, but unfortunately, the house was too well built. The yelling was barely audible outside.

Joseph, though, knew immediately something was wrong. His aunt had just bid them good night. He ran into his pa's room, where Charley slept when watching them and shoved one of her pistols into the back of his waistband. Then he heard the three girls file down the stairway. Emily rubbed her eyes sleepily. A chill ran through Joseph when he saw who was holding his aunt.

Aramus chuckled at the glare the boy gave him. He drew his pistol and slipped the knife back in his sheath. He told Charlotte to seat them on the long sofa. She placed them all down and Joseph showed her the pistol. She pretended not to see anything, but it gave her hope.

"Now come here," he commanded. He sat down on a chair opposite the children and stared at her. "Now," he said, "take off thet apron and dress."

Tears started flowing down her cheeks. "Please, let the children go back upstairs. I will do anything, but let them go up. They can't escape."

He said, "Do what Ah said."

She looked at the children. "Whatever happens, children, whatever you see, just try to put it out of your mind. Just remember some people you meet in life are sick, very sick like this man. Don't worry about me."

"Shet yo mouth and take off them clothes, now!" he said angrily.

Joseph said, "No, she won't. Drop it."

Aramus looked at the gun in Joseph's hand. Though he was surprised, he grinned, saying, "Boy, look the way mah gun is pointed. Ef'n you shoot me, Ah shoots her. Ef'n ya even kills me, Ah'll still pull the triggah. Yo drops yo gun."

Joseph said, "No. If I drop this, you'll kill her and us. If you hurt my aunt, I will kill you. You killed my ma. If you think I won't kill you, you're wrong, mister."

"Whooee!" Aramus said, laughing nervously. "Yo thinks yo is a big man still, don't ya, boy?"

"No, but I am."

Aramus whirled around and saw Chris Colt standing in the doorway from the kitchen, a Colt Peacemaker in each hand. Man Killer, slightly behind him to the left, also held a Peacemaker in each hand. Behind Man Killer a trapdoor from the storm cellar stood open. The two men had seen him from the window.

Chris Colt said, "Aramus Randall, you are under arrest for the murder of Shirley Colt, for the murder of an unnamed cowboy in Wyoming, near Rock Springs, a husband and wife in Jackson, Wyoming, and for attempted kidnapping and rape. Drop your gun. You're going to hang."

Though frightened, Aramus said, "Cain't do thet, Marshal. Same thing I tole yo boy. Ef'n ya kills me, mah bullet takes yo sistah through the heart. Now, sets yo guns down. You, too, boy."

Chris said, "Joseph, toss the gun on the chair over there."

Joseph knew he had to listen to anything his pa said. He threw the gun on the empty chair in the corner.

Charlotte said, "Shoot him, Chris."

Aramus, grinning, said, "You do, she dies."

Charley said, "He killed Shirley. Shoot him."

Aramus said, "Yo better not. She's gwine ta take one in da heart no matter what, less'n yo drop yo guns afore Ah counts ta three. Ah gots nothin ta lose."

Charley said, "Kill him. Forget me, Chris."

Chris said, "No." Looking at Randall, he

asked, "What if we set our guns down? What will you do?"

"Ef'n ya lays yo guns down, Ah gives mah word Ah won't hurt yo sistah or the chilluns. Jest yo."

Colt said, "What about Man Killer?"

Aramus said, "No, Ah is gwine ta kill him and yo, but Ah will let the chilluns and yo sistah live."

Colt said, "No, let Man Killer go, too."

Man Killer said, "No, here."

He tossed his right gun to Aramus, who tucked it in his waistband, and then his left gun.

Man Killer said, "I will die with you, Great Scout. The children and Charley must live."

Colt dropped both guns on the floor. He raised his hands and so did Man Killer. Aramus started laughing.

He said, "Yo fools. Now I kin kill ya all easy, but first Ah is gwine ta tie yo all up, so's ya kin watch yer sister an' me have a party. When Ah gits ta you Colt, Ah's gwine ta takes yo skin off a strip at a time."

He was laughing hard when suddenly the window shattered and Kuli, bowie knife sticking out of his side, flew through the air, his teeth sinking down onto Aramus's left arm. The force toppled the killer to the ground. He screamed as the wolf's fangs tore through his flesh and crushed the bones in his forearm. This was a wolf who could break the spine of a moose with the force of his bite, and Kuli knew he was protecting members of his pack. He growled and jerked and twisted and Aramus's left forearm and hand came free from his arm and Kuli slid across the floor, arm still in his teeth. Charley took two steps and dived across the living room.

Chris reached up behind his back and pulled out his bowie as Aramus drew his from the sheath on his gun belt. He started his throw first underhanded and the blade flew by Chris Colt's face, but it also threw him off balance and he slipped on the rug. Aramus dropped to the floor and grabbed one of Man Killer's guns and swung toward Charley, who crashed into the chair, holding her gun and went over with it. Lying upside-down and looking backward, she raised the gun and fired into the killer's chest. She rolled over onto her knees and stood up, as Aramus started raising Man Killer's gun.

Speaking while she fired, Charley put another round into his chest and drove him backward, saying, "You killed my sister-in-law. You would have killed these children."

He looked down at the spreading blood on

his chest and belly and the blood spurting from his arm.

She fired again, saying, "You monster. You don't deserve to hang. You don't deserve to take another breath."

Man Killer's gun started to slip from his fingers as she raised her gun and shot him between both eyes. He flew backward through the porch window, landing half outside on his back, his legs twitching in death.

Chris, both guns back in his hands, ran outside and made sure that the man was dead. He came inside and found Charley holding all four kids and Man Killer holding Charley. Joseph and Brenna ran into their father's arms and he hugged them closely.

Then Colt let go and everyone ran over to Kuli while Colt and Man Killer extracted the bowie knife and plugged the wound with a kerchief. Tex and several cowboys burst through the door, guns in hand, and whistled at the sight.

Colt said, "Tex, hitch up a buckboard with two of the fastest team horses we've got. Come on, Man Killer."

Colt stood, carrying Kuli in his arms, and Joseph ran up beside him, saying, "I'm going, too, Pa." He didn't ask. He stated it.

Colt said, "Grab some blankets, son."

They went outside, and minutes later, Tex came flying through the barn doors in a small buckboard and slid to a stop. Colt, Joseph, and Man Killer climbed into the back of the wagon, laying the big wolf on the blankets Joseph brought out. Tex directed a cowboy to run to Westcliffe and fetch the sheriff, and the undertaker. Colt told the man to take War Bonnet. Chris started to say something to Charley, but she waved him off and smiled at him bravely.

Colt looked down at his little boy, the night wind whipping through his blond hair as the wagon tore down the Texas Creek Road toward Westcliffe.

Chris said, "Kuli will be okay, son."

Joseph looked up and said, "I know it, Pa."

EPILOGUE

The sun was bright and the sky was almost cloudless. A pair of golden eagles swirled lazily on the thermals coming off the slopes below.

Chris Colt and his little boy looked at their bobbers out on the water. Several rainbow trout broke the surface farther out. Lakes of the Clouds was their favorite spot to go fishing.

Joseph yelled, "Kuli, come here!"

The big wolf had his head halfway down the hole of a marmot. Down below, they could see the tops of trees where the timberline ended and above them all around rocky slopes thrust up hundreds of feet.

Joseph said, "Pa, if we hadn't had that fight like we did with Aramus Randall, would you have shot him?"

Chris looked at the two eagles and back at his boy. "No, son. I would have manacled him and would have taken him to jail."

Joseph said, "But he murdered Ma."

Colt said, "I know that, son. I don't believe that any man could ever love a woman as much as I loved your ma. I'll never be able to love like that again. I tell you, I wanted to burn him alive, but this country needs men who treat the law as something bigger than themselves. We cannot live our lives by making up our own laws as it suits us. To be free men, we have to be willing to make laws for ourselves, and then have the courage to use those laws to make our lives civilized."

"What does civilized mean, Pa?" the little boy asked.

"It is one of the two things that makes us different from the animals, son."

"What's the other?"

Colt put his hand on his son's shoulder and said, "The ability to reason, to figure things out for yourself."

"What if someone tries to attack us?" Joseph asked.

"Then you have to defend yourself. That's okay, son. That's the proper thing to do, but only if we're attacked," Colt said.

"What if someone's making fun of me or teasing me, Pa?"

Colt said, "The best law to make for yourself is this. If you aren't sure, just try to love everybody as much as you can. And before you love anybody, son, love God first."

"What if I do that, Pa?" Joseph asked.

Colt smiled at his son, tousled his hair, and said, "Then you'll become a man."